THE REASON

THE REASON

Sandra M. Colbert

THE REASON

Windy City Publishers
2118 Plum Grove Road, #349
Rolling Meadows, IL 60008
www.windycitypublishers.com

Published in the United States of America

ISBN:
978-1-941478-31-8

Library of Congress Control Number:
2016944175

WINDY CITY PUBLISHERS
CHICAGO

For Carol Siwinski,
a true friend,
whose encouragement led me to where I am.

ACKNOWLEDGEMENTS

Oddly enough, I've never been in a police station or involved in anything, other than the occasional speeding ticket, that required the assistance of law enforcement. So my thanks to Verle Leard of the Harvard Police Department, for reading the initial manuscript and for giving much needed advice.

And fortunately, I've never been involved in a house fire. So my thanks to Chris Adlington of the Blue Island Fire Department, who was also kind enough to advise me on all things fire related.

And danke to Ruth Hannenberg, my friend of many years and my advisor on all things German related.

To my family and friends—they who plowed through an initial manuscript riddled with misspelled words and faulty grammar, then followed up with the words of encouragement that kept me going and continue to keep me going as a writer—my sincere gratitude to you all.

To my editor, Ashley McDonald, who does all that a good editor should do. And more. Words finally fail me.

"DETECTIVE HARRISON, HOW CAN I help you?" Paul Harrison asked irritably, annoyed by the interruption of the phone call.

"I need a homicide detective."

He smiled when he recognized his wife's voice.

"Why, Kate, you insatiable slut. Wasn't last night enough? I can only do so much," he said slowly.

"No, really, Paul. I need a homicide detective," she replied.

He heard the serious tone in her voice and sat up a little straighter. "What's going on?"

"The guys working on the new fence just found a body."

He was silent for a moment. Then, "Be there in ten."

"Okay everyone, listen up. You're all invited to my house," he said to the other detectives in the room. "Turns out I have a body in my backyard."

The other detectives all looked up at the same time, including his Captain, Ed Silverman.

"I wouldn't miss this for nothing." Ed grabbed his jacket and followed Harrison out of the station. He was joined by Roger and Kelly, the two other detectives in the office.

"We're right behind you, Captain," Roger said.

When the four of them converged on the Harrison's backyard, they found Kate at the rear of the property, wrapping crepe paper streamers around branches stuck in the dirt.

"Kate, what are you doing?" her husband asked, looking at her handiwork.

"Securing the crime scene."

"It looks like we're having a party."

"I don't have any crime scene tape. This was the best I could come up with."

All four detectives looked down at the remains in the earthen space. Most of the body was still covered in dirt, the remnants of a blue blanket that was used to cover him could be seen. The skull and most of the upper torso were exposed. The body lay facing up.

"How do you know it's a crime scene?" Roger asked. "Sometimes people just do weird things with dead relatives."

"The bullet hole in the skull was a hint," Kate stared down at what remained of the body. "Come see."

Roger knelt down to take a closer look. "Yeah, that looks like a bullet hole, all right."

Kate had been a cop for thirteen years prior to her marriage to Paul. There wasn't much that she hadn't seen. A bullet hole in a skull of an old corpse didn't unnerve her.

Paul looked around his backyard. The three Hispanic workers who had found the body were still there, standing at the opposite corner of the property.

"Someone tell them that they can leave," Paul said when he saw them.

Ed and Kelly walked over to them.

"You guys can go. Nothing else to see here."

He got blank stares.

"Understand. Vamanos, scram, agua caliente."

The workers looked at each other with confusion in their eyes. They gathered up their tools, and then headed towards the gate leading out to the front yard.

"Captain, do you know what you just said to them?" Kelly asked.

"Yeah, I told them to leave."

"Where did you learn your Spanish from?"

"A little something I picked up in my travels."

"Uh, you just told them 'hot water.'"

Ed shrugged.

"It worked. They left, didn't they?"

They walked back over to the grave.

"So, what do we have here?" Ed asked.

Kate was the first to speak.

"Middle-aged man, very popular in the community, very outgoing. Sold cars for a living and was very good at it. A bit on the heavy side, but took his wardrobe very seriously."

"Alright, enough Sherlock," Ed interrupted "Where did you get all that from?"

"He has a '1959 Salesman of the Year' tie clip on what remains of a nice looking tie. So he had to be loud and outgoing to sell cars and he must have made some great deals to be the salesman of the year in 1959."

"Showoff," Paul said with a grin.

"And he worked for Sullivan Ford, which is still in business."

Paul smiled and shook his head. His wife never failed to amuse and amaze him.

"What else did you come up with?" he asked her.

"His name is George Schumacher."

"And you know this how?" It was Kelly's turn to ask.

"Before we bought the house I researched the previous owners. The Schumachers lived here from 1947 to 1980. At least the wife and daughter did."

"They had a daughter?"

"Yeah, I also looked up census records."

"No wonder you're a PI. You're just plain nosey. And you don't know for a fact that this is George," Ed interjected. "By the way, did anyone call Forensics?"

"I did, Captain," Kelly replied.

"Anyone besides Kate got something to say?"

This time it was Paul who spoke up, as he knelt next to the grave.

"Mind you, this is just my observation, based on my many years of experience in crime detection," he said.

"Another comedian I don't need," Ed replied flatly.

"It was a woman who did it. Possibly a frail man, but I'm leaning toward a woman. The grave is shallow. The bullet hole looks like an exit wound, so he was shot in the back of the head. She dug a shallow grave, because either, physically, she wasn't able to dig very deep or because it was late in the season and the ground was starting to freeze. She did what she could then flipped him over and covered him up."

"I concur," Kate said.

"Why, thank you, Mrs. Harrison. Coming from an experienced PI such as yourself, that means a lot," he said.

He stood up and wiped the dirt off of his pants. "But let's see what Forensics comes up with."

"By the way, where's Nathan?" he asked Kate, referring to their recently adopted teenage son.

"At school, then going straight to work at the restaurant. He'll be home late."

"Good, I don't want him seeing this. It could end up all over the Internet."

"Paul, he wouldn't do that. He's got better sense."

"Yeah, I guess so. I hope so."

"How come nobody found this sooner?" Ed asked the group. "Hell, if this has been here since, what 1959 or 1960, you'd think someone else would have found him by now."

"It's near the corner, and part of him was covered by a bush, a lilac bush or something. We've been digging it all up to put in the new fencing," Paul responded. "Hell, I think this is the first time I've even been in this part of the yard for any length of time. It's a big lot."

"Anything else from the peanut gallery?" Ed asked the other two detectives.

"Gosh, there are roots coming out of his eye sockets," commented Kelly.

"Yes, well, how about something not so obvious and more constructive."

"How do you know he was overweight?" Roger asked Kate.

"His belt is still somewhat intact, and it looks like a good size one."

"Okay, I see that now."

"By the way," Kate said to Roger, wiping her hands on her jeans and reaching out to shake his hand. "I don't think we've met. You're the new guy on the team."

"He's our rookie," Ed interjected. "Roger Miller, King of the Road."

"Actually, Mrs. Harrison, its Mueller. Captain keeps calling me Roger Miller and referencing some song I had to look up by some old singer from ages ago."

"Hey, you should be flattered. Great song," Ed said, walking away singing the tune.

Kate looked over at her husband, who was definitely in his detective mode: hands on his hips, his eyes darting all over the scene and their backyard.

Paul had a reputation as one of the best detectives in the county. He was tough when he had to be and compassionate when he had to be. And doggedly determined, on whatever case he was working on, to get the job done. Her feelings of pride, as well as the incredible love she had for him, never diminished.

"You guys hungry?" she asked all of them. "I've got ham and cheese and rye bread. I can make up some sandwiches while you wait for Forensics."

"That sounds great. I'll have one," Ed was the first to respond, followed by Kelly.

"Count me out," said Roger. "I still haven't got to the point where I can eat at a scene."

"Well, you better get used to it, Rook," said Ed. "Otherwise you're going to go hungry a lot of the time."

"What about you, Hon?" she asked her husband.

"Ah, yeah, okay," he said, snapping out of it momentarily. "Hope they get here soon. I really don't want this guy here longer than necessary."

Kate went in to make the sandwiches while the others meandered around the area surrounding the gravesite.

Roger followed her into the house.

"Anything I can do to help?" he asked.

"Yeah, there is some iced tea and soda in the fridge. Would you find out what they want to drink?"

He came back shortly and started filling glasses.

"So, how long have you lived here?" he asked.

"A little over four months. My dream house always was a two-story colonial and I got my wish with this house. It was built in 1940. It even came with a little library that doubles as my office. We moved in this past March, did a lot of remodeling, so it's just the last couple of weeks that we don't live in a construction zone. We're moving on to what we need to do outside and now this."

"It all looks good. Great job," Roger said, looking around the stylish kitchen. "You guys been married long?"

"Since last October."

"You know he's a legend on the force."

"Yes, I know," she said smiling, but inwardly cringing. She knew what it took to become that legend.

"How long have you been on the force?" she asked.

"Eight years. I made detective three months ago. And I really hate being called the rookie. I think I paid my dues."

"Well, you know cops. They need to find something, about anything, to amuse themselves. It keeps them sane," she added, "I used to be a cop. Thirteen years in Phoenix, before moving back to the Midwest."

Roger was surprised. "Really? I didn't know that. The two of you must have some interesting conversations over dinner."

"Yeah, we do. We really do," she said thoughtfully. "So you better find something to laugh about or you'll lose it. Especially when you become a detective. Don't let it bother you, Detective Mueller. It's all part of the job."

"The Captain is a real character though. He keeps making references to stuff and I have no idea what he's talking about. I spend a large part of my day googling his comments so that I know what he's trying to say to me."

Kate laughed as she finished up with the sandwiches.

"He's a really good detective. He's also a good friend, and he'll stick by his guys, come hell or high water. I've seen him in action. Be glad you got him."

"You sure you don't want a sandwich?" she added.

"Yes, I am very sure."

"Then let's take these out there and feed your fellow detectives."

She glanced over at Paul as she handed a plate to Kelly. He was on the phone, pacing near the grave site.

"He called Forensics," Kelly said to Kate. "Putting pressure on them to make it fast."

"Come up with anything else?" she asked after they were all seated on the patio.

"No," Ed said with a mouth full of food. "We need Forensics here before we can go any farther."

"They're on their way," Paul said, finally hanging up his phone and grabbing his sandwich.

Kate saw Roger walk over to the grave, while the others began eating. She knew, instinctively that this would be a case that would get under the skin of the entire team. No one around this table could stand the thought of someone getting away with murder and this was a definite possibility with old cases.

A few minutes later Brad Steiner, the coroner, and his team entered the backyard.

"Uh, are we having a party or what?" They heard him say when he saw the crepe paper streamers.

"Don't knock it," Ed said, walking over to the grave, carrying his sandwich. "It's the new and friendly crime scene tape. Originated in Los Angeles. The citizens love it. Makes homicide more cheerful. Takes the sting out."

"And just what do we have here?" Brad asked, squatting down by the body.

The detectives joined Brad and his team. Ed and told him all that they and Kate had surmised until that point.

"Very good, Officers. I don't know why you need us."

"For starters, I need you to get this out of my yard," Paul said.

"You live here! This is priceless," said Brad, looking around at the property. "You know the place is haunted now. You released his soul when you dug him up."

"Yeah, whatever," Paul said "We'll deal with his ghost. I just don't want another old case sitting on my desk or a skeleton in my backyard."

"No weapon found, I suppose," Brad responded.

"Oh wait. Hold on!" Kate ran into the house and returned carrying a metal detector. "Here, use this."

"We own a metal detector?" Paul asked Kate.

"Yeah, I bought one when I bought the other private investigator toys. There's even more stuff. I'll have to show it to you someday."

"Uh, yeah, okay."

The detector began beeping almost as soon as the technician turned it on. They dug a small space near the body and came up with a gun wrapped in a decaying rag.

"That was too easy," Brad said as he examined the dirt filled and rusted gun. "It's a German Luger. Probably from before World War II. Strangely enough, I've seen several of these in my time. I believe it's safe to say that it's the murder weapon. I'll know more later on after I spend some time on it."

"Did this guy serve in the war?" Paul asked looking at Kate.

"Hey, I could only do so much. Vet's records are tougher than you think. Oh, by the way, his daughter works at the library."

No one said anything. They just looked at her.

"Please elaborate," Paul said.

"I just remembered where I've seen that last name. I'm in the library all the time and the name on the librarian's office, well, is Schumacher. Lolita Schumacher. Small town like this, it's got to be her. Her age would be about right. I spoke to her once, and she's probably the crabbiest librarian I've ever met. And I've met a lot of librarians."

"So, Ed, you want me to take it from here?" she asked Ed, just for his reaction.

"No, we are perfectly competent detectives and can handle the occasional cold case. He's not going anywhere. No rush. We don't need the services of a private investigator."

"Okay, just let me know when you change your mind," she said with a smile. "And since it's in my backyard, I'll even do it pro bono.

"Keep Sonny and Cher out of this," Ed replied.

"What?" Roger asked. "I'm confused again."

Just then Ed's cell phone rang. Paul's rang at the same time.

"This can't be good," Kelly said.

After a few seconds, Ed said, "Bank robbery in town. Let's hit the road, gents and lady. What is happening to our little affluent community?"

"Two banks," Paul said, when he ended his conversation. "Hit at the same time. They want us to stretch our resources."

"Kate, stay here with Brad. Find out what you can. It'll be a while before I get their report," he added as he leaned over to kiss her. "I have a feeling it's going to be a long day."

"Okay. Be careful. Love you."

"Love you, too."

As she watched them all run to their cars, she got that familiar sick feeling in her chest. Thirteen years as a cop, but it was only now that she was on the other side that she understood the stress it put on her former husband and the people who cared about her. Paul was an experienced cop and knew what had to be done when faced with a situation. But she also knew all the experience and caution in the world wouldn't stop a bullet. It didn't before.

"Please come back to me, my love," she said out loud as she returned to the backyard grave.

She watched as Brad's team took pictures, swept away the remaining dirt, and put the remains of George, as she now thought of him, in the body bag.

"Anything else, Brad?" she asked the coroner.

She knew him as well as she knew all the detectives on Paul's team. She had gone to him in the past with forensic questions. Brad admired her and wasn't reluctant to share information with her.

"No, not really. Shot in the back of the head. From the trajectory, I'd say he was kneeling when he was shot. That makes it a very cold and callous kill. No other items found. All very neat. Initially, from what I can see here, no signs of a struggle. I'll find out more when I get him on the table. "

Kate gave him a nod as she began to wonder how this was all going to end.

"Lot of questions to be answered," he continued, "But I do enjoy the occasional cold case. They're fascinating. Hope we can solve it."

"Me too," Kate said. "Hope the department here kept good records. He had to have been reported missing. He had a job and a family."

"As much as I hate to say it, maybe the family knew he was here," Brad said.

They both remained silent as they looked at the now empty space that once held George and his secrets for so many years.

"I really hope not," Kate said after a few moments. "That would be a worst case scenario."

"And besides, I really don't want to live with a ghost, figuratively or literally speaking," she added. "We've got to wrap this one up."

"Good luck with it," Brad replied. "I hope no one got shot in the bank holdups today. I'd rather deal with a 50-plus-year-old corpse. I'll do all I can to help."

"Thanks, Brad. I know you will."

"I'll be in touch with Paul as soon as I have more information to share," he said as he followed his team out to the waiting coroner's van.

AFTER THE TEAM LEFT, KATE walked slowly towards her house. She looked back one more time at the excavated corner of the backyard, which now had real crime scene tape around it.

"Time to get started," she said out loud to a nearby squirrel. He looked at her and scooted off.

She went to her office and took out a new notebook. In spite of the knowledge that she had with computers, she always hand-wrote her notes. It added clarity and pacing she didn't get when typing on a laptop.

But before she could finish her notes, she knew what the next step was. She looked out of her living room window at the Victorian house across the street. Hard at work on the roses in her front garden, was her neighbor, Virginia. From previous conversations, Kate knew that Virginia kept a sharp eye on what was going on in the neighborhood. So she had to have seen the cars and the coroner's van. At the same time, Virginia was also too polite and proper to come knocking on Kate's front door to make inquiries.

Kate knew Virginia would be a source of a lot of information, since she lived in this area all of her life.

She headed for the big Victorian house across the street.

"Hi, Virginia."

"Oh, Kate, hello," Virginia said, as she stepped away from her roses. "Looks like there was a lot of commotion at your place earlier."

"Yes, Virginia, there was. And there were also two bank robberies in town today."

"Oh dear. How dreadful. What is going on in this world? It all makes me so afraid."

"Would you like to take a break and come over for some iced tea?" Kate asked, looking at the picture perfect roses. "I'll fill you in on the situation. And I think you'll be able to answer a lot of questions that have suddenly come up."

"Yes, of course. Give me a few moments to wash my hands and lock up. I'll be right over."

Fifteen minutes later, Kate was serving Virginia iced tea in the living room. She knew this was something Virginia would appreciate. Virginia came from an old, established, and well-to-do family. She was raised to be a proper lady, during a time when that was important, especially in an affluent community. She once told Kate that she went to finishing school. At the time Kate had no idea what a finishing school was and had to Google the term.

"So do tell," Virginia said. "I mean four detectives and a coroner's wagon. Really dear, something big is going on."

Kate couldn't help but smile. Virginia was definitely observant.

"I don't want to keep you in suspense. But I need to ask you some questions first. How long have you lived in your house?"

"All of my life. My parents bought that grand old lady in the early forties. I was literally born in that house. Midwife—no hospital. I was born in 1948. Daddy was a lawyer in town. A very good one, I might add, and mother came from old money so they had the grandest house on the block. Although, I must admit, it is a bit much for me now. But I simply can't imagine living anywhere else. "

"So you knew or still know just about everyone in this town and on this block."

"I do know a lot, which would be normal for someone who has been here for so long. I have seen a lot of changes."

"Tell me about the Schumachers."

Virginia didn't seem surprised that Kate knew the name of her long gone neighbors.

"Well, there is quite a bit to tell there. They moved here in the late '40s. Probably 1947. I say that because their daughter Lolita was born the same year that I was born. We were playmates as little girls. The parents were very nice. Germans. Left after the war and all that horror. Not much in the way of accents though. And they really didn't want anyone to know that they were Germans. Said that they were Austrians. I found out much later that they were German. They were probably afraid that they would be treated with hostility. I'm sure that they wanted to spare Lolita any unpleasantness." She sipped her tea before continuing.

"She was quite spoiled, that Lolita. I just adored her father though. What a nice man he was. So funny and outgoing. He sold cars at Sullivan's. He was liked by everyone. That's why it's even more ridiculous when I think of what happened."

"What happened?" Kate asked.

"Well, that's just the thing. No one knows. He just disappeared. The talk was that he picked up and left his wife and daughter for another woman. I didn't believe it for a minute, even as a child. He was such a doting father and a loving husband. I can still see them at a wedding that we went to. He was dancing the polka with his wife. A wonderful couple. They were always so happy. He loved his family and this community. He volunteered for every event that this town had. He was even Santa for the Christmas Parades. There simply is no way that he took off with some other woman. There has to be more to it."

"Virginia, I believe that we found him."

"What do you mean?"

"You may want to put your glass of tea down."

After she did, Kate continued.

"This morning when the workers came to install the new fence, they came across a body. We believe it to be George's.

Virginia gasped and covered her face.

"Oh dear Lord, no. How awful. Oh no. Oh no. Does Lolita know?"

"Not yet, so please don't say anything to anyone. This still has to be confirmed. And it's the police who should tell her."

"Of course, of course. May I ask, how did he die? Was it foul play?"

"The only reason that I'm sharing this with you is because the press will probably find out about this, and of course, the police will eventually be around asking you questions. And I think you can probably help with the investigation since you knew the Schumachers," Kate said.

She took a deep breath and continued, "He was shot in the back of the head."

"No, no, Oh no. Who would do such a thing to such a nice man? Oh heavens," she crossed herself. "I was just a child. I don't know how much I really know. I don't know if I can help you. Oh heavens, How awful." Kate noticed that Virginia's hands were trembling and gave her a little time to calm down and absorb the news before going on.

"Virginia, I know that I told you that I worked at home as a CPA. But actually, I'm a private investigator."

"Really? I've never known a private investigator," Virginia said, after regaining her composure. "I guess I thought that they were something out of movies and books."

Kate had to smile. "We're real, Virginia. Trust me, we're real."

"And you know that my husband is a detective on our police force," she added. "It's just information that I don't like to share for a number of reasons. So please don't tell anyone else. But I do want to get as much information as I can get on the Schumachers."

"Aren't the police going to investigate?"

"Yes, but it won't be a priority. Especially after today, with two bank robberies in the area and God knows what else. They're going to be busy with current crimes."

"I see. Of course. I'll do what I can to help. Oh my! This is so incredible. Who did you say found him?"

"The workmen who came to install the new fencing."

"I bet that ruined their day."

"Yes, I'm sure it did, and it means that the word will get out soon. So please, ignore any reporters that come by and let the police handle them. Otherwise they will make your life a misery if you so much as answer a single question."

"Of course, of course. What can I do to help?"

"Tell me what you do remember about the time that Mr. Schumacher disappeared. What time of year, what was Lolita and her mother telling everyone about this woman that he supposedly took off with?"

"It was October, 1960. That I remember quite well. It was my birthday on the fourth. I turned twelve, the same age as Lolita. Although we didn't see too much of each other during that time. We seemed to outgrow each other. We started going with different groups as children are apt to do, especially as you approach the teen years. Different interests." She paused and frowned.

"Word spread that Mr. Schumacher hadn't shown up for work for a couple of days. I heard my parents speaking about it. His wife said that he was sick, but she could only lie for so long. She finally told people that he left her and Lolita, for another woman, no less. She said he left a letter and some money saying that he fell in love with this woman and was going to live in California with her. He would send them money every month, and she should file for divorce. He wouldn't contest it.

"I can remember how shocked my parents were. They knew the Schumachers well, and of course, they viewed this as total nonsense. So did the whole town. And I don't mean to make disparaging comments about Mr. Schumacher, but he was hardly Cary Grant, if you get my gist. He was a bit overweight and balding and had a funny nose. And he just adored his wife and little girl. It was ridiculous. The police even came around and asked questions, but she stuck to her story. She even said that she burned the letter. So there was nothing that they could do. Eventually, the talk stopped and he became a fond memory."

She continued, "Oh, Kate, this is so terribly sad."

"Yes it is," Kate said, and truly meant it.

"Do you think Martha, his wife, did it? Is that even possible?" Virginia asked, wide-eyed.

"I have no idea. Hopefully it will all come out now. It would be nice to give him a proper funeral and repair the damage done to his memory and legacy."

"Oh dear. I feel sick to my stomach."

"I know it's a lot to take in. Would you rather go home, or do you want to tell me more?"

"Kate, I'm only sixty-eight. I haven't reached my dotage yet. No need to treat me with kid gloves. I'm tougher then I appear. And I want to help in any way possible." She paused. "I'd like to see where he was buried."

"I'm sorry," Kate replied. "But it's a crime scene and I can't take anyone back there until I get the okay from the police. I'm not even supposed to go back there."

"I see, of course," Virginia replied.

"I have such fond memories of playing in this house as a child," she continued, looking around the room. "Even in the winter, Lolita and I and some of the other girls in the neighborhood played upstairs in the attic. There was a cabinet filled with all sorts of toys and things. We had such good times. My parents were so fond of George and Martha. They were such lovely people. And for a while there, when we were very young, Lolita and I were inseparable. It all became so tarnished over the years, and now this."

With a coldness in her voice, she said to Kate. "You have to find the damn bastard who did this."

"I'll do what I can, and I know the police will as well."

"Like you said, they'll put this on the back burner. You have to solve this. You have to. And you can count on me to do whatever I can to help this poor, poor man."

"For right now, just make notes about what you remember—about the times and about Lolita and her mom. I'll need some photos, if you have any, of George and the family." Kate said. "We can get together tomorrow and go over everything. I'll be doing my own research. Whatever I find out I have to turn over to the police. I just want to make sure it's as detailed and accurate as it can be.

"It is the daughter, Lolita, who works at the library, right?" Kate added.

"Yes, it is. Unlike her parents, she turned out to be a very unpleasant person. I never understood why," Virginia said. "But, yes. I can do what you asked. Oh dear, I think I just turned into Miss Marple."

They both laughed as they headed for the front door.

"And please…" Kate said.

"I know, don't say a word to anyone. I promise I won't. Besides, you don't know Lolita. I wouldn't want to be the person who has to tell her. And I certainly wouldn't want her to know that I'm involved in any way."

"Until tomorrow, Virginia."

"Until tomorrow, Kate."

IT WAS ALMOST NINE WHEN Paul walked in, looking as exhausted as Kate thought he would be. Throughout the evening she tried to watch TV or work on her notes but reached a point where she couldn't concentrate on anything. She just wanted to hear the garage door open. He called to say he was on his way, but she knew she wouldn't relax until she saw him.

"Hey, babe," he said, as he leaned over to kiss her,

"Hey, yourself," she said, returning his kiss. "Hungry?"

"Starving."

"Give me your jacket and relax. There's some cold chicken and potato salad. What do you want to drink? Beer okay?"

"Yeah, sounds fine. I'm so friggin' tired I may not have the strength to finish a meal."

"Tell me what happened today." They once made a pact to share what they could and not bottle things up, no matter how bad the situation was. He began to give her some of the details of the two bank robberies.

"I actually had to run and chase down one of the bastards."

"Did you catch him?"

"Yeah I did. The little shit is sitting in a cell tonight. The other three morons got away. But not for long," He shook his head in thought. "It was the running that was hard. I'm getting too soft. I'm sitting behind that desk too much."

"Paul, you work out a couple of times a week. You're in great shape for a…"

"Oh, please say it," he grinned. "I dare you. For a man my age? Go on. I dare you."

"You are in great shape for a man of any age. You're not even forty yet. And I speak as someone who has benefitted from, uh, your manhood," Kate said, with a smile. She stood up, went over to him and massaged his shoulders. "Relax and eat. You've had a long day."

"Is Nathan home yet?"

"Not yet. He's working at the restaurant tonight, so he'll be late."

"God, how does he do it? School all day, working in a restaurant kitchen at night. That's brutal."

"He's tough and seventeen. He's doing what kids can do at seventeen. I'm proud of him. He's keeping up with it all."

"Are you going to fill him in on today's find, or did you already?" Paul asked.

"No, I'd rather tell him in person and not on the phone. He's going to be sorry he missed all the action," she said. "And I'm not going to tell him tonight. I'll wait until the morning."

"So what else did you find about the deceased?"

"Well, our neighbor, Virginia, from across the street is a wealth of information," Kate replied. "But you don't really want to hear about it now, do you? You're exhausted. And you've had to deal with enough for one day."

"Yeah, you're right. Fill me in in the morning. Right now I just need a shower and some sleep," he said as he stood up. "Oh, and why did you call me on the outside line this morning, instead of my cell?"

"You big dope. It was an official call, and the calls coming in are recorded, right? I wanted the time, etcetera to be noted. I knew it would be a murder investigation."

"Hmm, and I called you an insatiable slut, didn't I?"

"Yes, you did. I really hope no one ever has to listen to that call."

"Well, it's not like it's not true."

"The whole world doesn't need to know," she said, after a long lingering kiss. "Besides it's your fault that I'm an insatiable slut. You're just too good in the sack."

"Enough, enough. I need some sleep and you're not making it easy. Now I have to take a cold shower. Go to bed. And you really don't have to wait up for Nathan."

"I know. I'll be up in a little while. I just feel better when I know my men are home." She kissed him again.

"Good night, love."

"Good night," he replied, kissing her on her forehead.

THE NEXT MORNING OVER BREAKFAST, she told Paul what she learned from Virginia.

"It's starting to sound like the wife did it and got away with it," he said, as he sipped his coffee.

"Can it really be that simple?" she replied.

"Sometimes it is. But usually not. Murder can be a complicated mess, as you know," he said. "I'm sure Ed will let you go with one of the guys to talk to the daughter at the library. That is the daughter, right?"

"Yeah, Virginia said it's her. She also said that she is unpleasant. Maybe she knows her mother did it and has lived with this knowledge," Kate replied. "It could be what made her so unpleasant."

"Could be," Paul responded as he put on his jacket and headed for the door. "Get together with Ed and see who is available today to break it to her. And make sure whoever it is gets a DNA sample. I don't want anything to get missed on this. And I really want this one put away. The press is going to have a field day and that field day will be at our front door."

"Yeah, I know. I'll do what I can," she said.

"Nathan still sleeping?"

"Yes, I better go wake him up or he'll be late for his first class. Plus I have to fill him in."

"Okay, later, babe," he said distractedly, already thinking about the workload on his desk.

"Later."

KATE WAS RIGHT ABOUT NATHAN'S reaction.

"Damn, I can't believe I missed all that!" he said in between mouthfuls of cereal. "A real corpse in our backyard. Wow, show me, and details, please. What did it look like?"

She told him what she knew so far.

"And it looked like a skeleton in rags," Kate said. "Not a pretty sight. Don't lose perspective. This poor guy was shot to death in his own backyard. He used to live here. He had a job and a family and a place in the community. He was well-liked."

"Hmm," Nathan said. "Apparently not so well-liked by someone."

"Yeah, I guess you're right about that," Kate said as she nibbled on a piece of toast. "And it is a crime scene, so it's off-limits for right now. I'll show you the grave when the cops tell me that I can. For right now you better get going. You'll be late for class."

"And please, Nathan," she added. "Don't spread the news about this to anyone. The press will be all over this soon enough. It can become a real media circus."

"Do I actually get to say 'no comment' if someone shoves a microphone in my face?"

"Yes," Kate laughed. "Be very emphatic about it too. The police department will handle the comments, so refer the press to them."

Nathan looked towards the now vacant, taped-off space and went silent. She could see that he was suddenly affected by the sight of the grave.

"It's pretty sad," he finally said. "Is Paul handling the case?"

"He and his whole squad are pretty busy right now, so I'm going to find out what I can. Something as old as this wouldn't be a priority."

Although, she thought, *the killer could still be alive and well and living a good life.*

"Let me know if I can do anything. Okay?" Nathan replied.

"Sure," she said, touched by his reaction. "Thanks, but you've got a lot going on. Try not to get too distracted by this."

"Yeah, but I hope you find out what happened," Nathan said. "Poor guy."

"Yeah, poor guy."

"So our house is haunted."

"Yes, in this one respect it is and always will be, regardless of the outcome."

AFTER PICKING UP A BOX of donuts, Kate headed for the station. Earlier she spoke to Virginia and was invited over to her place to have lunch with several of her friends.

"I know that you said not to tell anyone, but I couldn't arrange this luncheon without dropping some information."

"I understand, Virginia. It's all right."

"I should have quite a bit to share with you by then," Virginia said in a cryptic manner. Kate knew that Virginia would make a great Miss Marple.

Paul was not at his desk when she got there. She headed for Ed's office after getting a round of applause for the donuts.

"I hope there are plenty of chocolate ones in that box," he said when she walked into his office.

"I see you have your priorities," she said. "Where's Paul?"

"Chatting with a client," Ed said.

She knew this to mean that he was interrogating a suspect.

"So you want to go with one of my guys and meet the daughter. You understand that you are not officially involved in this, so you keep your comments and questions to yourself. You don't let anyone think that you are one of us. Though I wouldn't mind it if you were."

"Thanks for the back-handed complement. I'll stay in the background and observe."

"Okay, take Roger Dodger and let me know what happens. He'll be thrilled. He's got a crush on you."

"Oh please, Captain. Can we keep it real?"

"Just go get him and report back to me after you see the daughter."

"Thanks. Why don't you just come over for dinner tonight, and I'll fill you in then?"

"Barbeque ribs?"

"Sure, why not?" she asked.

"And beer."

"Only if you buy it."

"I better. I wouldn't want to drink any inferior beer that you may end up getting," he said. "You talked me into it. See you later."

A SHORT TIME LATER, KATE and Roger walked into the town's sleek modern library just as they were unlocking the doors. As always, Kate wondered what happened to the old Limestone and brick buildings that used to house libraries. She missed them. The new libraries offered so much more—but lacked the history, as well as the warmth and feeling of continuity that the old libraries had.

Lolita Schumacher was easy to spot. She looked out of place in the modern surroundings, with her grey hair pulled back in a severe bun, no makeup and a nondescript loose fitting dress. She was thin, almost too thin. Her skin was dark and leathery; her facial features sharp and angular. She was inspecting some books on a cart.

Roger showed her his badge and said he needed to speak with her.

"What about?" she asked curtly.

"Can we go to an office where we can have a private conversation?" he asked.

"Who's she?" she asked pointing to Kate.

"Can we find an office first?" Roger replied firmly.

"Fine," she said, not making any attempt to hide her annoyance.

She called over another library employee—a young girl, and gave her instructions on what to do with the books on the cart. The girl nodded and said nothing. But Kate could see a touch of fear in the girl's eyes."

"Come with me," she ordered Kate and Roger.

"Told you she was a crab," Kate whispered to him as they followed her to the back of the building. Her office was opposite the bathrooms. Her nameplate was attached outside the door, which is why Kate knew the name.

Her desk was a cluttered mess of papers and books that appeared to have been piling up for years. The dead houseplant on a file cabinet behind her completed the look of neglect and inattention.

She took her seat behind the desk without saying a word.

"This is Kate Harrison, a private investigator. She's assisting the department with this investigation," Roger said.

"You people now need a private investigator to help? Are you all incompetent? Is this what you spend our tax dollars on?"

Roger ignored the remark and gave her the address of her previous home.

"You were raised in that house. Correct?"

"Yes, what of it?"

"Miss Schumacher, a body was found on the property yesterday. We believe it may be the body of your father."

"That's absurd," she responded, without any display of emotion. "He left us when I was a child. He took off with some woman and went to California. We never heard from him again. He probably died out there. Not that I care."

"I know this is coming to you as a shock, but we have every reason to believe that the body that was found is George Schumacher, your father. He was found in a shallow grave in the corner of the lot."

"I'm not shocked and I repeat. That's absurd. He went to California," she said, still not registering any emotion.

"There is only one way to find out for sure. I need a swab from you for a DNA test."

"Are you all incompetent fools? I just told you what happened."

"I repeat, Miss Schumacher, we need a DNA swab to find out for sure. I would think you would want to know as well. Don't you want to know the truth?"

"It's probably the body of some homeless transient, a bum."

"Like I said, we have enough to indicate that this is not the case. All we need is a swab from the inside of your cheek, and if it is a match, we'll have the definitive answer."

"And like I said earlier, this is absurd." Kate noticed how tense Lolita was now getting.

"I didn't come here to argue with you. If necessary, I'll get a court order." Kate knew he was bluffing.

"Fine, what do I have to do?" she asked tersely.

"I just have to swab the inside of your mouth, and we'll be out of here."

"Be done with it and leave. I have work to do."

Roger took out his plastic gloves and the DNA sample kit from his jacket pocket. Lolita remained silent, giving Roger a steely stare as he approached her and asked her to open her mouth. Although she complied, Roger had the fleeting thought that she just might bite his finger off.

"We'll contact you with the results as soon as possible," he said after taking the sample.

"So with this discovery, I suppose everyone in this wretched town will now have something to talk about."

"Yes, Miss Schumacher, I'm sure there will be a lot of that," Roger responded softly.

There was no response, other than her hard stare.

Roger and Kate didn't speak until they got into the car.

"Okay," Roger spoke first. "Was that the weirdest, strangest interview ever?"

"Yes, yes it was," Kate responded. "She didn't even ask the cause of death."

"That's probably because she knows what it is," Roger said shaking his head.

"She gave me the creeps," Kate said.

"Me too."

"Fill Ed in, and I'll have my lunch with the lady across the street. I'm sure she'll have a lot to tell me."

"Keep me in the loop."

"Will do. Ed's coming over for dinner tonight. Feel free to join us."

"I may just do that. It would be nice to see your place without a corpse in the backyard."

KATE HAD JUST ENOUGH TIME to run to the supermarket and get what she needed for the dinner that evening. She freshened up and put on a skirt and blouse before heading for Virginia's house for lunch. There was something about Virginia that always made Kate feel underdressed and messy. Maybe it was because Virginia always looked and acted very much like a lady of a different era and class.

There was only a thirty year age difference between her and Virginia, but it was the class difference that Kate felt so acutely. Kate came from a small town in southern Illinois and was raised in a doublewide trailer. Virginia came from money and, for decades, her family maintained a certain amount of prestige and influence in this area. It was an insecurity that Kate could not get past, in spite of her fondness for Virginia and the friendship that was developing between them.

When Virginia opened the door, Kate was glad that she had changed into that skirt and blouse. Lunch was being served in the formal dining room and attended by two other people—an elderly, well-dressed woman and an older gentleman, who was also quite well dressed in a sports jacket and slacks. He stood when Virginia and Kate entered the room.

After introductions, Virginia added that both guests had worked with George at Sullivan's car dealership prior to his disappearance. The lady, Rose Cummings, ran the office and was secretary to Carl Sullivan, the owner of the dealership. The gentleman was Harold Simmons, one of the salesmen who had worked with George.

"This is incredible. Do you really think its George that was found?" Harold asked, after the lunch began and Kate had filled them in on some of the details.

"It appears to be. He had a 'Salesman of the Year' tie clip. And so far, Forensics hasn't found anything to rule out that possibility," Kate replied.

"He was such a nice man," Rose said, looking up from her curried chicken salad. "Everyone liked him. I simply don't understand."

"How long did you both know him?" she asked.

"I started there in 1954," Harold responded. "We had a friendly competition going—you know, to see who sold more cars. We were tied a lot of the time. But I did get that tie clip a few times."

"He started there in 1950, or maybe '51, I believe," Rose said. "So I guess I got to know him quite well in years that we worked together. I never believed, deep down, that he would leave his wife and daughter. He simply wasn't the type."

She paused to take a drink of her iced tea. Kate noticed that the iced tea glasses were Waterford.

"He adored his wife and daughter," she continued thoughtfully. "My, how he doted on that little girl. She was extremely smart for her age. She could even speak and read German. George and Martha had taught her. She was always reading. No surprise that she worked in a library all these years."

"Does she know?" asked Virginia.

"She was told this morning," Kate said. "She totally rejected the idea that it could be him. She was still sticking to the story that he abandoned them."

"I would think this would be a preferable scenario," Harold said. "Unpleasant as it is."

"The police did get a DNA swab, so we'll know for sure in a couple of days," Kate said. "What can you tell me about her and her mother?"

The mood suddenly shifted as the three of them took an interest in their lunch. Kate felt a tension creep into the room. No one looked up until Kate spoke again.

"Lolita was very unpleasant when we went to speak to her. Was she always like this? So angry and, well, rude."

Rose spoke up first. Her cheeks reddened. Now there was anger in her voice.

"They spoiled her rotten. Whatever Lolita wanted, Lolita got. And George, he just bragged about her so much. Such a nasty child."

"She was a very smart little girl for her age," Virginia interrupted. "She was always the smartest in the class. She seemed, well, even when we were so young, to be so driven to get perfect grades. She simply had to be the best in class. As it was she had the best clothes and the best dolls—she simply had to be the best, to stand out. Looking back, she was very unusual. Much too serious for a child. She wasn't fun to play with because she always had to win. And she always had to be the boss."

"Virginia, you're a bit generous in your description of her," Rose interjected. "She was a brat. Pure and simple, a spoiled brat."

It took Harold to move the conversation in another direction.

"The wife, what was her name?" he asked.

"Martha," Virginia said.

"Yes, Martha, very meek and quiet, but pleasant, always pleasant. I remember her bringing pastries to the office for all of us," Harold said.

"Yes," Rose said a bit calmer now. "I remember that as well. Those little pecan pastries. They were delicious. What a funny thing to remember."

"What about after the disappearance?" Kate asked.

"Well," Rose spoke up first. "They became very reclusive. Mr. Sullivan always had company picnics and Christmas parties. And he always invited them. But they never came. They wouldn't even return our calls. They just lived in that house, the two of them and cut themselves off from everyone."

"Yes, I remember that as well," Harold said. "I went over there shortly after the news and offered to help with home repairs or anything that they might have needed. Martha practically slammed the door in my face. Even years later, it never changed. If anything they just seemed to get even more antisocial, Lolita more so than her mother."

"That's right," said Virginia. "Lolita's grades never suffered, but she became more of a loner. It was like she hated all of us. Like it was our fault. She hasn't changed much, unfortunately."

"What about high school?"

"Her grades were so good that she ended up in classes way ahead of me. She got her diploma earlier than the rest of us. And of course, she never attended her graduation ceremony. She went away to a small college, we heard. Out near Skokie. That only lasted a year or two, then she came back and got the job at the library and has been there ever since."

"What about boyfriends? It's a small town. There would be talk."

They all looked at each other and shrugged.

"Not that I was aware of," Virginia said.

"Me either," Rose added.

"But like I said, they got very reclusive," Virginia said.

"What about the mother? Did she work?"

"Oh yes," Rose said.

"Even before the, um, incident, she worked part time at the Woolworth's downtown. She did go full-time and eventually became a manager. And, yes, I would say she remained pleasant. At least to me. Quiet, not talkative, but somewhat pleasant. Unlike her daughter. That girl was so filled with venom. I could never figure out why. I know thinking that your father abandoned you can be an awful thing, but Lolita was and still is, well, simply put, a pure bitch."

"Nobody would argue with you about that, Rose," Harold responded. There was a distinct sadness in his voice. "It makes you wonder what George would make of her if he was around today."

"When did Martha die?" Kate asked.

"In 1980," replied Virginia. "Heart Attack. Once again, it was all veiled in secrecy. If it weren't for the fact that she worked at Woolworth's we probably wouldn't have even known about it. Lolita had a very small funeral without the traditional luncheon afterwards. No wake, of course. It was shortly after that that she sold the house and moved away."

There was a thoughtful stillness in the room. Harold pushed his plate away and shook his head at the memories he was now confronting.

Rose and Virginia also stopped eating and appeared lost in thought. Kate chose to not interrupt them.

"I'm afraid we're not shedding too much light on this mystery that you are faced with, Kate," Virginia was the first to speak.

"No, you are. You have to remember I'm not from around here, so I have a lot of gaps to fill in," she replied.

"When Virginia invited me over and told me what it was about, I got to thinking," Harold said. "Well, the memories started to flood back, as they do at this age, so I'll tell you something that I remember quite clearly.

"At one of the annual picnics, all of us guys were sitting at a picnic table, drinking beer, and as was usually the case, we started putting away a lot of beer. George was there, and George loved his beer. Some of the guys were World War II vets and someone brought up the war and one thing led to another. That's when George told us his story. He was a bit drunk or maybe a lot drunk. Someone asked him what he did in the war. He suddenly told us all that he was a German. He told us that he was in London during the war. He said that his parents sent him there in 1938 when they saw what was happening in Germany. He was only 11 when they sent him away. He told us that his parents hated Hitler, and they were not about to see him become a Hitler Youth and end up fighting with the Nazis. They stayed behind and he never saw them again. He got all teary eyed when he was telling us about it. They sent him to live with a banker in London. Apparently, his father was a banker in Berlin and had worked with this London banker over the years. He lived with this banker's family and at times worked at the bank as a translator, if they needed one. He even translated for other British people. Even though he was a just a boy, sometimes the officials, according to him, asked him to translate documents. That's why his English was so good and his accent was hardly noticeable. This banker's family treated him like one of their own, and after the war, they were the ones who got him to America. He went to live with a German family in Chicago, went to vocational school there, and then got a job as a car mechanic. That's where he met Martha. She was a waitress at a German restaurant. She was a German war refugee. They got married, moved out here, and he ended up selling cars. He said he loved being around cars."

"I remember that," Rose exclaimed. "He was not one to get drunk at the work functions, but he did at this one. It was talked about almost by everyone the next day."

"That was probably the most that he ever said about his life before moving here." Harold went on, "But it was unlike him. Especially when he started to cry. He sobbed actually. Martha came over and got him and the three of them left a short time later. We could never get him to talk about it again. He would just change the subject."

"It's funny that I didn't know that. My parents were pretty close to them," Virginia said. "Lolita never even mentioned that to me. But then again, it wasn't the kind of things children would talk about."

"Well, the other reason that I remember it all so well was because of Lolita," Harold said, frown lines forming around his eyes. "She was there near the table, hovering. She always seemed to be hovering. When she heard her father tell this story, well, she just glared at him with what can only be described as unbridled hatred. It was Lolita that got her mother and insisted that they leave. But the way she looked at that poor man just made me so angry. She had no right to show him such disrespect in public. Awful child, just awful. I still don't talk to her when I see her in public, not that she cares."

"When did this happened? Do you remember what year?" Kate asked.

"Oh yes, I remember. It was the last picnic that they went to. Labor Day, 1960," Harold responded. "It was shortly after that when George disappeared."

KATE DECIDED TO WAIT UNTIL the four of them finished eating the ribs and the corn on the cob to go over what she had learned earlier. She was still trying to work it out in her mind.

"Compliments to the chef," Ed said, wiping his mouth on yet another napkin. "All made from scratch, I assume."

"If you call unwrapping the package and sticking the ribs on the grill— making them from scratch, then yeah, it was made from scratch," Paul said.

"And I boiled the corn and opened the can of beans," Kate said "And yes, I can cook. I just don't have the time, what with crime fighting and private investigating and all."

"Well, it was still very good," Roger said. "Thank you."

"You're welcome, Roger."

"Where's Nathan?" Ed asked.

"At the restaurant, working," Paul said. "He only gets two nights off a week."

"He still taking GED classes?"

"Yeah, he's almost done and then he starts culinary school in a few weeks," Kate added. "He's trying to make as much money as he can for the tuition. It's expensive, and he doesn't want to take money from us. We've offered, but he wants to do this on his own."

"He's a good kid," Ed said. "You got lucky."

"I know. And he'll turn out to be great at this. He really loves to cook," Paul boasted. "He's already talking about owning his own restaurant someday."

"Between him and Terrance, I hardly get to use my new fancy kitchen," Kate added.

"I didn't know that you wanted to use it," Paul said to Kate, feigning surprise. "Aside from coffee and sandwiches."

"Very funny, dear. And you may want to share your own culinary expertise with the group," she said.

"Hey, I'm the master of the microwave. I'm quite skilled when it comes to zapping."

"Yes, of course, I almost forgot about that. You are good at pushing buttons," she replied with mock steely stare. "Anyway, who wants dessert? I have some great vanilla ice cream and chocolate sauce. Then I'll fill you all in on what I learned about our friend, George, and his family."

As they ate their ice cream, Kate told them what she learned in the course of the day.

"I know it's a stretch," Kate said, notebook in hand. "But..."

"But?" Paul asked.

"But I think this has something to do with World War II," she replied while doodling in her notepad.

"You're stretching this like a rubber band, my dear," Ed responded. "I think the mother did it. The kid witnessed it and has been keeping it a secret all these years and went a little batty because of it."

"Ed could be right on this one," Paul said.

"Could be?" Ed asked with raised eyebrows. "They had a fight. Maybe he was a closet drinker. Things got out of hand and she shot him. Sometimes, it's the quiet, timid ones that are bottling up too much and then one day they lose it. He may have been an abuser. We see it all the time, Kate."

"I know, I know," she replied. "But it's the way he died. Very much like an assassination. Back of the head, he was kneeling. Only one bullet shot from a steady hand. Very cold and calculated. And with a Luger."

"That doesn't change anything," Ed said. "She could have been planning it for a while. He knelt down to pick something up, pull up some weeds, maybe dig up a bottle that he had stashed and—bang! It's sometimes easier if you're not looking at the victim in the face."

"And the gun?"

"Hey, they were German. Who knows what kind of souvenirs they brought with them. It's not like there was a TSA back then."

"How long have you lived around here?" Kate asked Ed.

"Been in this part of the state a good fifteen years. I started in the force downstate, in Springfield."

"Have you ever met her?"

"No, but I don't get to the library too often."

"That's obvious," Roger said softly.

"What was that, Rook?" Ed asked Roger with a slight smirk.

"Nothing, Captain," Roger responded. "But there's only one way to find out for sure what happened. Let's go ask her."

"Spoken like a true detective," Ed said.

"You think she'll talk after all these years?" Paul asked.

"Who knows?" Roger replied. "Maybe she's sick of carrying around this secret and will spill what she saw. Then end of story. It's not like we could arrest her or her mother. She may talk. Though she is one strange piece of work."

"She sure is," Kate added. "From what Virginia and her friends said, she's always had a mean, nasty streak, and from our short conversation with her, she was amazingly cold, not to mention rude. Her reaction was just plain weird. Hard to say how she'll react to more questions, especially if we hit her with a positive DNA ID."

"But on the other hand," Paul said, "Kate could be right and someone showed up out of his past. Someone with a secret that he shared with George. If this kid was translating documents for years during the war, he may have stumbled on to something. He could have just stayed in England after the war. How did he end up in a small town in the middle of the United States?"

"Oh, great," Ed said. "We have an international incident on our hands? I don't think so. I think you guys are watching too many movies. Usually the simplest answer is the right answer."

"Roger, when do we get the DNA results?"

"We should have them tomorrow."

"Fine. As soon as you get them, go see the lady at her home. She had time to absorb what you told her and may have a more normal reaction."

"Okay, will do."

"Take Katie here, and, Paul, you go with them. Paul has a way of asking the right questions. He'll teach you a few things. Plus he scares the shit out of people."

Kate looked at her husband and thought back to her first meeting with him. "Really? Paul? Scary? Hmm, that's news to me."

Paul just smiled back.

"She'll probably try to seduce me," Paul said. "Just like you did."

Kate threw her pen at him. "Oh really? Please, let's not rewrite history, Detective Harrison."

"Oh, ugh! Can we please change the subject?" Roger asked. "Paul, you haven't seen this hag close up. And I had to see her real close up to get the sample. She gave me the creeps. I was afraid that she'd bite my finger off."

"Okay, kids, I've heard enough for one day," Ed said as he stood up to leave. "I'm off like a dirty shirt. See you all tomorrow with a statement from this citizen that'll put an end to all this nonsense. Hasta la leggo, and thanks for the excellent dinner."

"I'm going, too," Roger said. "I'll let both of you know when I get the DNA results. And thanks for dinner. It was great."

"Yep, see you guys tomorrow," Paul said.

"YOU'RE NOT BUYING THE MOTHER scenario?" Paul asked Kate as they were cleaning up after the meal.

"I don't know," Kate said. "That's probably what happened. But it just seems like there are a lot of unanswered questions about the whole family. Or maybe Ed's right and I'm just complicating things. It's just a gut feeling that there's more to it. And Lolita is just so weird."

"Well, hopefully, we can have the answers tomorrow. I really hate the thought of this dragging on," Paul said. "When are the fence guys coming back, if ever?"

"Next Tuesday, if it's all right with your Police Department. Then I thought we would put something where the grave is, like a bird bath and some flowers. I'm trying to erase the "grave" image that we all have in our heads."

"Yeah, I know what you mean. It'll be a tough image to shake, and something tells me it'll be a topic of conversation anytime anyone comes over. Has the press been snooping around?"

"I've seen some cars slowing down, but no one's been knocking at the door yet, but I haven't been home that much either," she said.

"Let me know if it gets crazy. I'll send a squad car around."

"Okay," Kate said as she struggled to stuff the dishwasher.

"What do you have going on tomorrow, besides coming with us to confront this lady?" Paul asked, taking over the dishwasher duty. Kate conceded, knowing that he was much better than her with this chore.

"I'm meeting Virginia at 9:00. She wants me to meet more of her friends," Kate replied, as she handed him some cutlery. "Now that the word has gotten out, I think a lot of the seniors will have a lot that they want to share about this family."

"Or a lot that they want to gossip about."

"We'll see. It could make for an interesting morning and maybe fill in some blanks," she said. "So call me when those results come in and I'll meet you and Roger. Then you can work your magic on our friend, Lolita."

"It is weird to know that she lived here," she added, looking around the kitchen.

She gave Paul the dirty bowls that she was holding.

Paul looked over at her. "Well, it was a different house and time. Glad we did so much remodeling. From what you told me so far, I don't think I want to picture her in this house, even as a kid."

Kate turned to look back at the corner of the yard, now shrouded in summer darkness. A shiver ran through her. She wrapped her arms around herself. The air around her was cold.

"Me either," she said so softly as to not be heard.

She turned back and watched as Paul finished up with the dishwasher and pressed the buttons to get it started.

"I miss Terrance," she said abruptly, not sure what brought this on, but the feeling of a sudden absence hit her.

He reached out and enfolded Kate in his arms.

"I know you do, babe. You hate it if he's gone for a couple of days and this is, what, week two? Has he told you when he's coming back?"

"He emailed me yesterday and said he didn't know. He's still helping his father with his uncle's estate and all those ghastly, grim details of death, as he put it. He said he hated leaving his father. His dad was having a tough time dealing with his brother's death. They were so close and both in their late seventies."

"Yeah, that's got to be rough, at any age. Lord, I can't imagine how I would handle losing my brother," Paul replied.

KATE AND TERRANCE

KATE ALWAYS FELT THAT SHE hadn't left Phoenix; she had fled Phoenix. She lived there for eighteen years, doing a thirteen year stint as a police officer and being married for four years before she was hit with a perfect storm of misery: a husband filing for divorce at the same time that her best friend was dying of breast cancer was emotionally brutal. But it was what she witnessed as a cop that finally broke her. One call in particular, on a heat smothered Phoenix night that left her with nightmares and the realization that, at best, justice was elusive. Too often, the bad guys just got away with it. And Kate couldn't live with that anymore and still do her job as it had to be done.

So she fled back to the Midwest, to the place that she knew. A familiar place of golden corn fields and pastures dotted with languid herds of cows. A place of cool summer nights punctuated by the glimmering blinks of lightning bugs. A place stricken with the intensity of blizzards and cruel, icy, winter days.

And to a job at a library in Rockford. And a new life in a duplex owned by Terrance Beck, her landlord.

At one level, Terrance Beck was the very stereotype of an English Professor. In his late fifties, he taught English Literature at the nearby university on a part-time basis. Short and slight of built, he favored fedoras and always wore a tweed sports jacket and a tie to class. Because Kate was an avid reader and lover of history, they soon spent many evenings discussing history, books, and world events. Terrance was also an excellent cook, so many of these conversations were held over delectable meals and fine wine. Before

SANDRA M. COLBERT   39

long and to her surprise, Kate found herself sharing with him details of her life that she rarely shared with anyone.

At this time in her life, when she never felt more bereft and alone, Terrance became the person that she needed the most in her life. He became her confidant and, when needed, he became her care giver. It was Terrance that she ran to with good news or when she needed a shoulder to cry on. It was also Terrance who could be harsh with her, if that was what she needed. He always seemed to know. He never let her down.

It was Terrance who was partly responsible for getting Kate and Paul together. And it was Terrance who shared his love of cooking good food with Nathan and began showing him the basics. Whenever possible, it was Terrance with Nathan at his side taking over the kitchen.

Paul genuinely liked Terrance. He knew Terrance would always be a part of their lives. He saw the deep affection that the Kate and Terrance shared for each other and was glad for them. Paul knew theirs was a bond that could not be broken. They had been through too much together.

Currently Terrence was in his hometown in the English countryside outside of Oxford. He had always been close with his family so the news of the sudden death of his uncle shook him and he was on the next flight to London.

Both Kate and Paul knew that Terrance was going to be sorry that he missed this. He loved a good mystery.

"DAMN! DAMN! DAMN!" KATE SHOUTED, as she unfurled the local paper. "Paul!"

"I'm right here! What?" he asked as tried to drink his coffee.

"Look at this!"

On the front page of the local paper, was a picture of their house with the headline, "Strange Case For Local Police–Former Community Leader's Skeleton Found in Backyard."

"Oh no. That's all we need," Paul said quickly reading the article. "I'll get a squad car out here. Does Nathan know not to say anything to anyone?"

"Yes, he does. Hope we don't need more than a squad car. Damn. They even mentioned that you're on the force," Kate replied reading over his shoulder. "I don't think there will be any shortage of people who want to talk to me now."

"There will probably be more than enough. I hate leaving the house empty," Paul said. "I think I'll stay home, at least for this morning, while you're out."

"Good idea. I'll go get dressed and get Virginia. Something tells me this will be a not-so-good day."

Virginia informed Kate that they were going on a drive and even insisted on driving, which was fine with Kate since they now had a squad car blocking their driveway.

"You have to admit, this is pretty exciting, Kate," Virginia said as she pulled out of her driveway.

"Ah, yeah, right. It's not your house or your backyard," Kate said as she watched a small group of people gathering in front of their house. "So where are we going?"

"We will be visiting with two of my friends who I went to grade school with and who knew Lolita quite well at the time," Virginia said, turning towards downtown. "We'll be meeting at Betty's house. Ellen will be there. They are both very nice."

"I'm sure they are," Kate said, looking down at the list of questions that she had written in her notebook.

"Oh, and reach into my purse. There are some pictures that I dug up."

Kate took out the pictures and began flipping through them.

"I'm afraid there aren't very many."

"No, this is good. Thanks."

All three of the pictures were in black and white. Judging from the hairstyles and the clothing, they looked like they were taken in the 1950s. The other two were school pictures. Virginia explained that the first two pictures showed Martha and George with Virginia's parents at different social functions. Virginia didn't know what the functions were. The third picture was of George and Martha only, taken in front of their house, now Kate's house. The last two were typical grade school pictures, the first one was a class of third graders and the last a class of fifth graders. Kate had no problem picking out Lolita. She sat in the front row with a small semblance of a smile and had her hands folded on the desk. The pictures were similar and Lolita was in the same seat with the same pose in both.

The pictures of George and Martha were poignant. In all of the pictures they had broad smiles on their faces and had their arms wrapped around each other. They looked happy.

Kate sighed and began to put the pictures in her purse.

"Is it okay if I hang on to these for a short time?"

"They're copies, so please, just keep them," Virginia said.

Betty had a small but nice ranch style home on the edge of town. As with Virginia, the place was nicely furnished and the dining room table was set with fine china and a nice selection of pastries. After introductions were made, Kate got down to her questions. She didn't want to appear rude but she was beginning to feel the stress of this situation.

"So ladies, what can you tell me about Lolita and her family? How well did you know her?"

Ellen began.

"Well, we were all in the same grade, but Lolita stuck out because she was so much more advanced than us. Or maybe, different, is a better choice of words for her. Until we were about ten or eleven, the four of us played together quite a bit.

"But then things started to change. Lolita started to withdraw from us and become more of a loner. But we still did some things together from time to time—going to the movies, that sort of thing."

"She was, without a doubt, the smartest kid in the class," Betty interjected. "Always had her nose in a book. But that's exactly why I stopped playing with her. And that's why my parents wouldn't let me play with her."

"What do you mean?" Kate asked.

Betty looked around the room at all of the women.

"I never shared this with either of you, but I'm not sure I even understood the significance of it at the time. My mother and father did. That's when they said I couldn't play with her anymore. Do you girls remember that?"

"Yes, I do," said Virginia. "But I never understood why."

"Me either," Ellen replied. "Not that I cared. By this time Lolita was just a mean little thing."

"How old are we talking about here?" Kate asked.

"I want to say we were eleven or twelve when things really changed."

"So what prompted this?" Kate asked.

Betty took a deep breath and continued.

"This sounds so weird even now saying this," she continued. "We had a science project where we had to partner up with another student, research and build something. We had to show how volcanoes work. I got stuck with Lolita. Anyway, I went over to her house one Saturday. Her parents were home. They were very nice people and they sent me up to Lolita's room. Her mom even offered to bring up some milk and cookies. So I walk in and Lolita is on the bed reading a book. It wasn't our science book."

She paused and seemed reluctant to continue.

"Go on," Virginia prompted.

"Like I said, this sounds so weird even today saying this. But it was a copy of *Mein Kampf*."

"Hitler's *Mein Kampf*?" Virginia asked, wide-eyed.

"What?" asked Ellen, choking down her coffee. "How on earth does an eleven-year-old get a copy of *Mein Kampf*, much less read it? I was still reading *Nancy Drew*, for God's sake."

"I know," Betty continued. "I had no idea what this book was, but when I asked her she went into this spiel about this great man, Adolf Hitler. I was still awfully young, but the war was recent enough so that even I knew that Adolf Hitler was an evil monster that started the war. It gets even weirder."

"It can get weirder?" Kate asked.

"She had a framed picture of Hitler on her nightstand. But when her mom came into the room with the milk and cookies on a little tray, she faced the picture down."

"After her mother left, she told me that she wished she could have been a Nazi Youth. At that point I changed the subject and tried to talk about the science project. We went through the motions of talking about volcanoes, but I just wanted to get out of there. We planned one more meeting for after school so that we could build that stupid volcano, but by that point I didn't want to have anything to do with her. When I told my parents about it, they told me to stay away from her. No argument from me. I went back to reading *Old Yeller* and *Little Women* and playing with you girls. I stayed as far away from her as I could. I still do."

No one said anything for a while.

Finally, Kate asked, "What were your feelings after you heard about the disappearance of her father?"

"You know," Ellen said. "I didn't give it much thought. I had distanced myself from her by then. Her father seemed like a nice guy. He used to be Santa Claus at the parade every year. I just let the adults talk about it and stayed away from her. And like Betty, I still stay away from her."

Betty added, "For me it was just another weird thing from this weird family. I didn't want to know about it."

"I already told you my feelings about her," Virginia said. "But this Hitler thing, even though I never knew about it, it was about this time that I started to stay away from her."

"Was there anyone, boy or girl, who remained friends with her?" asked Kate.

"Hard to say. She kept on winning awards, and before you knew it she was in high school while we were still reading *Nancy Drew*," Ellen laughed.

"And getting interested in boys," Betty added.

"No boys that you know of for Lolita?" Kate said.

"If there were we didn't know about it. But I do remember a lot of jokes about her when that movie with James Mason came out," Virginia said. "Believe me, I'm not just being catty, but she was no movie 'Lolita'. She looked very much then as she does now, with the pulled back hair and the plain dresses. No makeup. Hard to say what kind of boy she would attract then."

"A Nazi?" Betty replied, and they all burst into laughter.

"Have you spoken to the Goldmans?" Ellen asked Kate.

"Who?"

"The people who bought the house from her after her mother died."

"Yes, yes," Virginia added enthusiastically. "That would be a good idea."

"Oh right. The man that we bought the house from," Kate said. "We never got to meet him. Mrs. Goldman had passed away, and Mr. Goldman moved to Florida, so the whole transaction was handled by his attorney. I never even spoke to him."

"I have his number. We keep in touch," Virginia said. "Not often, but enough. I think I'll have him give you a call."

"I would appreciate that."

"Do you know for sure that it's her father?" Betty asked. "The papers are sure they know who it is."

"Yes, I know. I didn't need to see a picture of my house on the front page this morning," she said. "The police are waiting for the DNA results. Hopefully we'll have them today, and we can give Lolita the news. From what we've seen so far, I'm convinced it's him."

"So you've spoken to her," said Betty. "How did she take the news?"

"Denied it. She would rather believe her father took off with someone else. She really is a very unpleasant person."

"So she hasn't changed," Ellen said.

"Doesn't sound like it," Kate said.

"STAY OFF THE GRASS!" KATE yelled at the people meandering on her front lawn, as she walked through the front door.

"Kate, you sound like an old man yelling at kids," Paul said walking towards her.

"Well, they're walking all over the new sod. Morons."

"Come here," he said as he wrapped her in his arms.

"This is starting to get to you, isn't it?"

"Yes, our house, our lovely house is being defiled. I can't stand it. I love this house."

"I know. I feel the same way. It'll stop soon. It's only temporary," he said. "But you're starting to really stress out over this."

"I know. I think because it is our house. I'd handle this better if it were someone else's house," she said. "What happened to me? I used to be a lot tougher than this."

"You're still tough. But we're just in the middle of something very out of the ordinary."

"I have pictures of them. Virginia had some old photos that she gave to me. They looked so happy." She paused. "God, I really hope we find out what happened."

"You will. You're a good P.I. I'm sure you'll figure it out."

"In the meantime, you wanna go upstairs and fool around?" she asked, slowly running her fingers up his chest.

Paul could only laugh.

"No, I can't believe I'm saying this but, no."

"No! Why no?" Kate asked, feigning shock. "You never say no."

"One—I have to get back to the station. I wasted the morning here. Two—Nathan is home and is downstairs watching a cooking show. Three—I just got dressed."

"Hmm—all of them lousy reasons," she said.

They were interrupted by the chirp of Paul's cell phone.

"Damn," Kate said as she walked away from him and sat on the chair in the foyer.

All she heard him say was, "Yeah, okay, yeah. Meet you in the parking lot." Then he hung up.

"Come on, my little private eye. Let's go."

"DNA was a match, wasn't it?

"Yep. I'll tell Nathan we're leaving."

TWENTY-FIVE MINUTES LATER, THEY WERE standing in front of a jewelry store on the town square with Roger. Lolita lived in the apartment above.

"Are we sure she's home?" Kate asked Roger.

"She works every Saturday. So this is her day off. I checked with the other people at the library," Roger replied.

"Well, let's get this over with," Paul said as he opened the side door that led to the upstairs apartment.

Lolita was standing in her doorway before they made it to the top of the stairs.

"So now there are three," she said.

"Miss Schumacher, this is Detective Paul Harrison," Roger said.

"I know who he is," she replied in her usual cool manner. "Come inside."

"I've done my research as well. You two are married," she said to Kate.

"Yes, it's not a secret."

"And you live in that house."

"You've read the paper this morning," Kate responded, trying to hide her dislike of this woman "I wouldn't call that research."

Paul slowly began walking around the apartment. It was a four-room, old style apartment with thick, dark woodwork and a transom over the entry door—a reflection of the age of the building. The living room was in the front with windows overlooking the town square. A small dining room was in the middle of the apartment, with the kitchen at the farthest end. The bedroom was off the dining room.

It was the furnishings that Paul found interesting. An armchair by the front window facing out of the room. Next to the chair, a TV tray that held only a set of binoculars. The rest of the room was furnished with a very basic sofa, another arm chair, a coffee table, a couple of floor lamps, and a small TV set in the corner. No pictures, no plants—no attempt at decorating. In the center of the dining room sat a card table and a single chair. The rest of the dining room was dominated by book cases, all totally filled with books. He didn't go into the kitchen or bedroom but focused on the bookcases, while listening to the exchange in the living room.

"I suppose, Detective Mueller, that you have news for me," she said, after turning away from Kate.

"Yes, Miss Schumacher," he said. "The results are positive. The man that we found is your father."

"Well, well," she said, not displaying any emotion. "I suppose I should arrange for a burial. Thank you for bringing me the news. When will you release the remains so I can get on with it?"

"It's not that simple, Miss Schumacher. He was shot in the head," Roger replied. "That makes it an open murder case. We have to investigate it. The murderer can still be out there. This will be investigated as if it were a current murder case."

"Don't be ridiculous, Detective Mueller. Who cares what happened fifty years ago?" Kate and Roger looked at each other. Before they could respond, Lolita continued.

"Are you of German Heritage?" she asked, still looking at only Roger.

Roger, somewhat shocked that she could be so disinterested in what he had just told her, decided to answer her with the hope that he could break through this shell.

"Yes, I am."

"I thought as much, when I heard your last name and saw your blond hair. Tell me about your family."

Roger looked at Kate and shrugged.

"Alright. My grandparents immigrated here in 1949. My Aunt Ruth was only eight months old when they went through Ellis Island. Her brother Ronald, my father, was born here. My grandfather passed away but my grandmother is still with us and doing very well at the age of ninety."

"Why did they do that? Why did they leave Germany?"

"Well, it was pretty bad after the war. My grandparents were looking for a better life. They had just gotten married and had a daughter. There was nothing for them in Germany. Many Germans, even years after the war, were still going hungry."

"You don't have to give me a history lesson on Germany. There isn't much that I don't know about Germany either before or after the war," she said. "Do you come from rural people? Did your grandfather and the people before him run a mill?"

"Yes, yes they did," he said. "They came from a town called Exter. Several generations of the family ran the mill."

"Of course they did. Muller is the name for millers. In America it's Mueller. It's nice that you've been able to retain the name," she continued. "Did your grandfather serve his country during the war?"

"Not in the military. He and my great grandfather were the only mill operators in the area and everyone needed the mill, especially in war time. From what I understand my great grandfather hated Hitler and the Nazis. I was told that he was somewhat vocal about it and probably would have been jailed or worse, if they didn't need the mill so badly."

"Why?" she asked. "Why did your great grandfather hate Hitler? Hitler did a lot of good for his country. He loved Germany and the people of Germany."

Before Roger had a chance to respond, Paul walked back in the room.

"I think we've had enough of the German history lesson," he said as he leaned against the door and stared down at her.

"Do you speak German?" she asked Roger, ignoring Paul.

"Yes I do. My father and my aunt spoke only German to their parents, so I learned to speak it as a child. I took German in High School and some courses in college. I also visited Germany a few times."

"That's good. That's very good," Lolita responded. She finally turned towards Paul.

"You're rather brusque and rude," she said, glaring at him. "Are you done snooping around my apartment? Next time, bring a search warrant."

"Miss Schumacher, your father was shot in the head," he said, ignoring her comments. "Doesn't that bother you?"

She was silent and once again, she displayed very little emotion. She looked down at her crossed hands on her lap.

Kate sensed that Lolita was using all of her energy simply to not to show any emotion.

"Do you know who killed your father?" Paul asked.

"Of course not. What a stupid question."

"Did your mother shoot your father?" he said. "You may as well tell us. It's not like we could arrest her."

"My mother? Don't be ridiculous. My mother was very meek, very gentle. What a stupid thing to say!"

"I think you know more then you're telling us. I think you know what happened that day," he continued.

"What utter nonsense." She began to look tense. Her eyes now darted around the room. "You have no idea what you are talking about."

Kate could see that Lolita was starting to react to Paul's questions.

"Please leave," she said forcefully. "Go do your job and get out of my apartment. All of you."

Kate and Roger looked up at Paul. He nodded and they stood up to leave.

"Doing this good cop, bad cop routine just reeks of amateur police methods." She directed her comments at Paul. "No wonder crime is on the rise, with incompetents like you on the force."

"I would watch what you say to us, Miss. Schumacher." Paul walked over and looked down at her. "The next time we won't be so considerate and will question you down at the station."

She once again looked down at her lap, her hands still tightly clasped together.

"I was a child, you fool. How do I know what happened?"

"You were twelve. Old enough to see and understand a lot of things." He continued, "Where there any strangers suddenly coming around the house?"

"No, there weren't," she said. "I came home from school, and my mother told me that my father left us for another woman. She was distraught. Of course, I believed her. What else could I believe?"

"Did you see the note that he supposedly left with your mother?"

"No, she said she burned it. She was extremely upset as I am now. So please leave."

Kate saw that Lolita was pressing her hands together so tightly that she was probably in pain.

"Danke, Fraulein Schumacher," Roger said to her.

She looked up at him. This brought out a small smile for the first time from Lolita. She nodded back at Roger.

"I guess the way to her heart is through Germany," Roger said when they were out in the street.

"She knows something. She probably knows everything," Paul said. "And we're back to square one."

"She's quite mad, you know," Kate said.

"You sound like Terrance," Paul said to her. "So please don't start quoting *Macbeth*."

"I'll control the urge," she replied with a smile. "Can we just get back to the station? I hate the fact that she is probably looking down at us with her high powered binoculars."

ON THEIR WAY TO THE station they stopped at a small deli and picked up some sandwiches, not forgetting to get one for Ed. They didn't speak about Lolita on the way to the station, but instead silently processed what had just happened.

"I'm going to call Nathan and see how things are at the house," Kate said as Paul parked the car. "Plus I think I need a Nathan and Kate day. Maybe we can plan something. I'll be in there in just a few minutes."

"Include me in that. It seems like I only see him when I pass him by in the house," Paul said. "Our lives are getting a little too scattershot."

After the call Kate joined them in Ed's office where his conference table was now covered with the sandwiches.

"Everything okay?" Paul asked Kate.

"Yeah," she said, unwrapping her sandwich. "But we still have morons walking on the grass. He's off tonight. Did you know that?"

"Yeah. Did you forget?"

"Yes, I did. I'm a lousy mother."

"Can we get back to the issue at hand?" Ed interrupted. "No confession, I assume. Your thoughts? Better yet, your solutions."

Kate went first and filled them all in on what she learned from the ladies at the breakfast. She started by passing the pictures around and then telling them about the *Mien Kampf* episode.

Their reactions mirrored the ones that the ladies had.

"You're telling me that this little shit of a kid was reading Hitler's manifesto?" Ed asked. "No wonder she's nuts. Just when you think you've heard it all."

"She is pretty hung up on Germany. She started on my last name and wanted to talk about all things German today," Roger interjected. "She could care less that her father was murdered. My family history was more important. Then she made that remark about what a great man Hitler was."

"Her book shelves were interesting," Paul said. "One whole—and I do mean entire bookcase—is devoted to Germany. Several Hitler biographies, including the one written by Toland. Travel books about Germany, books written in German, dozens of books about World War II. She is probably quite the authority on the subject."

"What about the other bookcases?" Kate asked.

"Mostly nonfiction. Accounting books, political books. Most of them looked old and outdated. She probably gets them from the library when they're ready to chuck them." He continued, "I'd like to take a better look at them, but I couldn't see anything that looked like a casual read."

"And the apartment is so austere," Kate said. "Not a single picture of anyone. No decorations of any kind. Just that pair of high powered binoculars."

She told Ed about the chair facing out and the binoculars on the TV tray.

"I could picture her looking down at the square when the farmer's market is going on or the art fair. Just spying on people, not participating. How lonely. How creepy."

Everyone was silent for a few moments.

"Roger, Paul, how many cold cases we got out there?" Ed asked. "Find out asap. Check the whole county. If he or she got away with this one, God forbid, there may be others out there that were committed by the same person. There may be some connections. Maybe this woman is just too afraid to talk."

"I didn't get that impression," Roger said. "I think she's holding out on us. And she's not right in the head."

"Yeah, whatever," he replied before anyone had a chance to say anything. "It's now a cold case. We got a lot of current crimes and miseries going on and not enough detectives as it is. And this is the one that will get all the attention."

"Kate work on this full time if you can," he added. "On the QT."

"I plan on it."

"Contact us when you really have to. Get us as many leads as you can. I need something to report to the higher ups. My guys have too much on their desks as it is, including your husband here."

No one said anything. Kate nodded.

"In the meantime, everyone get out of my office. I have a meeting in a half hour with some senior official about this guy George."

They silently cleaned up the table and walked out of the office.

"God, what's with him today?" Kate asked Paul as he walked her to the car.

"Pressure is getting to him," Paul answered. "He doesn't handle it well when a story hits a front page and he has nothing to report. He's afraid it will become more than a local story, and frankly, so am I. He has to answer to the higher ups. So do what you can, Kate. I really do have a lot going on and I have to be in Chicago tomorrow to testify on a case. Wish I could do more to help you."

"Don't worry about it. Just get me what you can on any other cold cases," she said. "Call me later when you're ready to come home. Nathan or I will come and get you.

"Yeah, okay," he said. She kissed him and watched him slowly walk away.

IT'S THE PICTURES, KATE THOUGHT on her way home. Seeing George and his wife in those pictures, looking so happy, got to her.

"George, I swear, I will find out what happened," she said out loud as she pulled into her driveway.

The squad car was gone, as she knew it would be. They could only sit there for so long. But gratefully, she didn't see anyone lurking around.

Nathan came bounding down the stairs as soon as he heard her walk in the front door.

"Hi Nate," Kate said, as always, just happy to see him.

"Hi Mom," he replied. He knew that she just loved it when he called her mom. It was, at times, a little tough to say since his biological mom hadn't been dead for very long, but he was starting to get comfortable with it.

"You just missed a phone call," he said, as he pulled a piece of paper out of his pocket.

"From who?" she asked.

"A Saul Goldman, from Florida." He handed her the paper.

"That was fast work on Virginia's part."

"Does this have anything to do with the dead guy?"

"Yes, it does," Kate said, as they walked into the kitchen.

She fished the pictures out of her purse and handed them over to him.

"And his name is George Schumacher."

"Wow, this really makes him real, doesn't it?" he replied, looking at the pictures. "Is that our house in the background?"

"Yeah, and everyone keeps telling me what a nice guy he was. I hope when this is all said and done that he is still a nice guy."

"Anyway, I think we all need a break from George for little while," she said to Nathan, taking the pictures back. She could see that the pictures were starting to affect him, like they did her. "Do you have any plans for tonight?"

"Nope, just hanging around here. Making sure no one walks on our lawn or looks in our windows," he said.

"Was there a lot of that after we left?" she asked.

"A little, but the cops scared them off," he said. "I'm getting a lot of emails and texts from people I hardly know. They want some kind of tour."

"Ghouls, the lot of them. What happened here was tragic," Kate said, now annoyed. "So ignore them. In time, they'll move on to something else."

"There was one weird thing though."

"What?"

"About an hour ago, some old lady, she just stood there on the sidewalk, not moving. Just staring at the house. Then Virginia came out and called something out to her, and she, like, took off down the street, real fast. She wouldn't even look back at Virginia."

"Was she skinny, with her hair pulled back and wearing a loose baggy dress?" she asked, already knowing the answer.

"Yeah," Nathan said. "Looked kinda creepy. You know who she is?"

Kate decided not to hide any of this from Nathan. He had a right to know.

"That was Lolita, George's daughter, their only child."

"Really. I wonder why she went practically running down the street when Virginia called out to her."

"She's afraid, Nathan, very much afraid."

"Of what?" he asked.

"That's what I have to find out," Kate said, looking again at George's picture.

Kate decided to call Saul Goldman in the morning. She knew she needed a break from George, and she knew that she would think more clearly in the morning. She told Nathan that the three of them would have dinner together. There was homemade lasagna, made by Terrance, in the freezer. She would make the salad and garlic bread. Lately dinner together didn't happen too often. After dinner they would rent a movie and just relax.

Nathan seemed pleased with the idea. "You sure you don't want me to make the salad and garlic bread."

"Very funny, but I think I can handle that part. I can even get the lasagna in the oven."

"Okay, catch you later. I've got some reading to do," Nate said as he left the kitchen.

But before any of that could happen, she updated her notes, while everything was fresh in her mind. Paul was right. Lolita knew something, probably everything. Kate had to find a way to get her to talk. That was the difficult part, the very difficult part. Something happened that traumatized her as a child and turned her into a cold, withdrawn, lonely adult.

"ARE WE HAVING COMPANY?" PAUL asked, when he walked in followed by Nathan and saw that the dining room table was set for dinner, with the good china and lit candles.

"No," Kate said, bringing out the salad. "It's family night, so I thought we would do it right and eat in the dining room.

He and Nathan just looked at each other and shrugged their shoulders.

"Okay," Paul said. "Kind of 1950s, but okay."

"Do I have to change my clothes and put on a suit?" Nathan asked, smiling at Kate.

"Just change the sweaty tee shirt. And wash up while I finish the garlic bread."

"And wine glasses for all three of us?" Paul asked.

"I thought a little wine would be good for Nathan to try. And you could probably use a few glasses," she said, pausing to give him a kiss. "I know I could."

"I guess I'll leave my tie and jacket on," Paul responded. "This is really very nice. Thanks Kate."

"You're welcome," she said. "Now pour the wine."

After the dinner and the cleanup, in which all three avoided talking about the situation that surrounded them, they went downstairs to the family room and began watching a movie. It wasn't long before Paul and Kate fell asleep. Nathan hurled throw pillows at them to wake them up when the movie ended and the local news was on.

"What a couple of old fogies. You missed a great movie," he said as they sat up.

"I saw the whole thing," Kate mumbled. "Give them all Oscars. Especially the sexy girl heroine."

"Which one?" Nathan laughed. "There was more than one sexy girl heroine."

"All of them. What brilliant performances by this all-star cast."

They stopped talking when the newscaster mentioned the 60-year-old cold case in their town.

Paul let out a groan and a few curses.

"This is going to get out of hand," he said. "We can't let them know that we've involved a PI, no offense. Somehow we have to free up Roger and Kelly to work with you."

"Did they pull up anything on the other cold cases?" Kate asked Paul.

"Yeah, I left it in the car," he said. "Nate, would you go get them for me? They're in the back seat."

"Yeah sure," he said, as he ran up the stairs.

Paul looked at Kate.

"I didn't want to ruin our family night."

"That many?"

"Too many. And don't let anyone know I took those out of the building. That could mean trouble for me."

"I won't. I'll give them back to you as soon as I can."

Nathan returned with what appeared to be a half of a ream of paper and handed them to Kate.

"So many? You've got to be kidding," Kate said, flipping through some of the papers on the top of the pile.

"Nope. I wish I was kidding. I'm off to bed," Paul said. "You coming?"

"No, I'm kind of awake now," she said, wide-eyed and looking at the papers in her arms.

"Darn, and I was going to take you up on that offer from this morning."

She hardly heard him as she sat down and wondered where to begin.

"Don't stay up too late, and thank you for the lovely family night dinner," he said. He kissed her good night.

"Yeah," Nathan said. "It was great. Even the wine. Night."

"Glad you enjoyed it," she said distractedly, "Good night, both of you."

KATE TOOK THE PAPERS UP to their library after stopping in the kitchen to make a cup of tea.

This can't be right. How could so many cases go unsolved? How could so many murderers get away with murder? This was the same conversation that she had with herself so many times in the past as a Phoenix cop.

Looking at this mound of paper just strengthened her resolve to find George's killer.

"George, you got to help me out here," she said out loud to the empty room "I've got to find out what happened to you and why, so if you can help in any way from where you are, I'd really appreciate it."

There was only silence.

"You got nothing George? Really? Hmm, guess I'm on my own," she said, taking out her notepad, then turning on her computer.

It was almost 2:00 am when Paul walked in the library and found his wife asleep and slumped over her computer.

"Kate, honey, it's two in the morning. Time to go sleep in the bed."

"Hmm, what?" she said, wiping the hair out of her face. "What time is it?"

"Almost two in the morning."

"What are you doing awake?"

"I don't know. It has something to do with sleeping with someone long enough so that you wake up when she's not next to you," he answered, helping her with her tangled hair.

"Let's get you in bed."

"I had a very productive night," she said in a groggy mumble.

"Really. And just what did you produce?"

"I read some of the stuff you brought home. Then I bought a really cute purse and a darling pair of shoes, and a little something for the house. I forget what."

"I hope that you didn't spend thousands of dollars." He had to smile. "Who knows what you paid right before you dropped off to sleep."

"No, I was wide awake at the time," she said. "And I did my research on Hitler Youths."

"Oh good," Paul said, shutting down her computer. "Just what you need to read before going to sleep. If you have nightmares, it's your fault."

"Hitler was not a very nice man," she slurred.

"So I've heard," he said taking his wife by her hand.

"He was very bad."

"Yes, yes he was," he said as he led her out of the room, pausing to shut off the lights. "You can stop talking now. I think you're still sleeping."

"I think so too."

THE NEXT MORNING, WHEN KATE came downstairs, she found two notes on the table, one from Paul and one from Nathan. They had both already left for the day. Both said that they would talk to her later. They probably left the house about the same time. She looked up at the clock. It was only seven thirty.

"*Damn,*" she thought as she poured herself a cup of coffee and got her toast going. "*Just what time did you guys leave?*"

After looking out of all the windows to make sure no one was lurking around her property, she grabbed her notebook and began to make a list of things to do that day that involved the case.

It was too early to call Saul Goldman, but not Virginia. Virginia once told her that she was always up by six.

She answered on the second ring.

"Virginia, would you like to come over for a cup of coffee?"

"I'll be there in a couple of minutes," she responded. "I'll bring the coffee cake."

Shortly afterwards, the two were sitting at the kitchen table and Kate was filling her in on what happened the day before.

"I can't help feeling sorry for her," Virginia said in between bites of coffee cake. "The binocular thing is rather creepy. I'll always feel her watching me now when I'm at the square."

"As soon as I start feeling sorry for her, it switches over to anger," Kate responded. "She knows something. She probably knows everything and she's not talking."

"It may be too traumatizing."

"That's a possibility. But does she really want to take it to the grave with her? And we may solve this on our own."

"Her appearance here after your visit does mean something, don't you think?"

"Yes, I think it does. Tell me what happened. How long was she standing there?"

"At least ten minutes. I kept looking out the window because of all those silly people milling about. I didn't want them on my property or bothering me. Then I saw her, just standing there. Not moving a muscle, just staring at your house, well, and her house once. I let her stand there for a good ten minutes, because I was afraid that she would run off if she saw me, and unfortunately that's exactly what she did."

Kate cut another slice of coffee cake for both of them.

"Well, we have definitely shaken her up. Now we need something to break down that wall that she's created all of these years."

"I can't get past that *Mein Kampf* thing. That age, the ten, eleven, twelve age, well, one is just so impressionable, sometimes permanently so," Virginia said. "Did she read it because the German title caught her eye? Did she know it was taboo and that made it all the more attractive?"

"Did they go to church?" Kate asked, suddenly switching gears.

"Yes, the Lutheran church, a few blocks from here. That's where she held her mother's funeral service."

Kate sighed and shook her head. Once again, she looked toward the corner of the yard. They both remained silent for a few moments.

"Well, I better leave you to it," Virginia said as she took her cup and plate to the kitchen sink.

"Yep, and I better return Saul Goldman's call. Thanks for contacting him for me."

"Oh, he was really interested in what's happening. He has a lot of happy memories of this house, so it bothered him that this happened. But I must say, he was relieved that it wasn't him that found George."

"Yeah, well, I could have done without it myself."

AFTER VIRGINIA LEFT, KATE HEADED for the library with her coffee and her notebook. She dialed the number Nathan gave her.

"Is this Saul Goldman?" she asked, when a man answered the phone.

"Why, yes it is. This must be Kate Harrison," he said. Kate could almost hear his smile over the phone.

"I'm so glad you called," she replied.

"So am I. I'm sorry that we couldn't meet at the closing, but I really didn't want to leave Florida for that nasty weather up there. I have some health issues. And my lawyer had it all under control. How is that great old house?"

"Well, right now it's a little frayed around the edges. At least the backyard is."

"Yes, Virginia filled me in. How awful. And to think we lived there all those years with a homicide victim in the backyard. You were installing a new fence, I understand."

"Yes and when one of the workers started digging and pulling up the old chain link fence, well, one thing led to another, and here we are."

"How can I possibly help?"

"I'm not sure myself. But please tell me what you can about living here and what you remember when you bought the house. Did anything strange ever happen when you lived here? Strangers asking questions, strangers lurking around?"

"No, no, nothing like that. That's something I would remember."

"So tell me about yourself. Where you born here? How did you end up in this house?

"No, I wasn't born there. Far from there actually, but my wife and I moved there right after we got married. Very typical, small town America. Good place to raise a family," he replied. "I was always in banking. By the seventies, I was an executive with Continental Bank in downtown Chicago. We lived in a ranch home on the edge of town for twelve years. Frankly, I was really sick of the commute to Chicago, so when a position came up at the bank here in town, I jumped at the opportunity. They hired me as a vice president, and eventually I became the president," he said. "I always admired that house. What a classic. But it was getting really run down over the years. So when it came up for sale, I was first in line. My wife felt the same way about it. We had two small boys, and it was close to the school and shopping. I didn't mind that it needed a lot of work. We wanted to put our touch on it anyway, which is probably what you've done, according to Virginia."

"Yes, we sure have," said Kate. "We love the house, too."

Kate looked around the room where she was sitting. She could picture a tall, handsome, older man, who could only be a bank president, in this room, choosing a book from the built in cabinets.

"Is that when you met Lolita? Or did you have any contact with her prior to that?"

"Oh dear God, Lolita. That's someone you never forget."

"Apparently. Please tell me what you remember about her."

"Where do I begin? It started even before we bought the house. When she found out that I was an executive at the bank, well, she had an account there, and she withdrew all of her money and didn't hesitate to tell people why."

"Why?" Kate asked, dreading the answer.

"Kate, let me ask you something first."

"Okay."

"Are you Jewish?"

"No."

"Have you ever met a truly anti-Semitic person? Someone who hates Jews so much that the hatred dominates their life?"

"I think I just recently did. Lolita?"

"Lolita. If she saw me walking down the street, she crossed over to the other side. If I went to the library, she ran in the other direction. Not that I cared. When you're Jewish, you come across this, even in this day and age and even more so then. There were Neo-Nazi marches in Skokie then. It makes me sick. But somehow you learn to deal with it. It was worse for my parents and grandparents. Just because you live in America, it doesn't mean that you won't get persecuted for being a Jew.

"So, according to my lawyer and my realtor, she went crazy when she found out it was me who was the buyer. She didn't want to sell it to me. But she had no choice. The county was going to take it for the back taxes that hadn't been paid. I guess her mother had medical issues before she died. And then there was the basic upkeep that they simply didn't have the money for. So she told everyone that would listen that I was taking advantage of her and practically stealing the house from her."

"That must have been an ugly real estate closing," Kate said, while taking notes.

"She didn't show up. Told everyone that she wouldn't enter a room if I was in it. So we signed the papers at different times."

"What kind of condition was the house in?"

"Pretty bad. We had an inspection done and knew that we would have to replace the roof, and the plumbing had to be updated. We changed the heating system and put in air conditioning. Carpets were shot. But here is what irritated me the most. The stove and refrigerator were fairly recent and in good working order when I had the inspection done. I planned on replacing them down the line, after the other things got done. But the day that we moved in, they were gone and replaced with dirty, shabby, broken ones. So there we were, on moving day, running out to buy a new refrigerator and stove. I was furious. There were the two young boys to think about. Horrid woman."

"Did you ever have any dealings with her mother?"

"No, not really. I saw her around town and my wife saw her at Woolworths. She was nothing like her daughter. Pleasant, but always a little sad around the edges. We just attributed it to the story of her husband running off on her." He continued, "As a matter of fact, she had a small account at our bank for years and never moved it."

"So there was no one popping up and asking for either of them after the sale went through?" Kate asked. "Was there a lot of mail that had to be forwarded? Anything like that?"

"No, nothing. But there is one thing…I just remembered."

"Yes." She sat up a little straighter.

"You know how when you move into a new place, you find little odds and ends that the previous owners left behind?"

"Yes, I know what you mean."

"Well, as my wife was unpacking and cleaning, she came across a number of things. Little things, a cookbook, figurines, nothing of value. But she thought they may have some sentimental value for Lolita, so she boxed them up. My wife was a very sweet and forgiving woman. We tried contacting Lolita at the library to tell her that we had them, but she wouldn't take my wife's call. So we left messages. My wife even went down to the library with the box and she refused to see her. So we gave up. We stuck it up in the attic, and as far as I know it's still there."

"It is?" Kate asked, picturing the large empty space. "I only poked around there briefly when we were moving in, but we didn't have that much stuff so we didn't need the attic space. We may someday. But I never saw any boxes."

"Did you notice the built-in cabinet in the corner? It's decorated with flowers and things like that."

"Yes, I did. I tried to open it, but the door was warped and I couldn't get it opened. So I left it for another day."

"Well, I shoved it in there. And as far as I know it's still there. I wasn't going to toss the stuff and have her tell everyone what a thief I was, which she was already doing. We should have thrown it all away. She didn't deserve such consideration, but like I said, my wife was a very forgiving person."

"So it should still be there."

"Yes, even when I was moving, my sons asked me about it, and I just said to leave it in there. Now you and you're husband can decide what to do with it."

"I'll go take a look as soon as I hang up."

"So tell me about the house and what you've done."

Kate filled him in on the remodeling that they had done.

"I had the library added on, you know," Saul said. "I loved that room."

"It's my favorite room in the house," Kate exclaimed. "I'm sitting in it right now."

"I miss that room. My wife and I spent many hours sitting by the front windows, just talking or reading. I'm glad that you're enjoying it."

"We are. Please come and visit us some day. I would love to have a real visit with you."

"I may just do that. The summers are brutal down here and I do get lonesome, and of course, I miss my wife. It's difficult to enjoy anything without her."

"We would love to have you as an overnight guest. I'm sure you have a lot of stories to share."

"I do. I really do and they are not all about Lolita, but I do have to mention something."

"What?" Kate asked.

"I hope you don't think I'm off my rocker or that I've got too vivid of an imagination, but..." he paused.

"But what?" she asked tentatively.

"Virginia told me that you're a private Investigator and that your husband is a detective."

"Yes, that's right."

"In September of 1977 there was a murder, a particularly bad one."

"Tell me about it."

"Well, at the time, there was no synagogue in the town. My family as well as the other Jewish residents in the town had to travel quite a distance to attend services. So there was talk of building a synagogue in our town."

"Okay."

"It was a Friday night, and one of the rabbis from Chicago was driving in to meet with several of us to discuss the matter. He never made it here. Just outside of town he was killed. Shot in the head while in his car. Then the car was lit on fire. No one was ever caught. Someone simply got away with murder. It was a horrible hate crime. Simply horrible. I've never really gotten over it. The police tried to downplay the Jewish motive for the crime, but I know that was the reason. I just know it."

Kate looked over at the stack of unsolved murder reports on her desk.

"How awful," Kate said. "No suspects?"

"Not that I know of. But I heard that when someone made mention of the crime, Lolita laughed. And from what I understand, it takes a lot to make Lolita laugh."

Kate felt a chill go through her body. They were both silent for a few moments.

"I'll look into it, Saul. I promise. I'll look into it."

"Thank you, Kate. I would appreciate it," Saul said. "And please send me pictures of you, your family, and the house. It would mean a lot."

"I will and I hope to meet you in person someday."

"Me too. Keep in touch."

"I will. Good bye, Saul," Kate said as she hung up.

SHE SAT MOTIONLESS FOR A few minutes. Then her phone chirped. It was Paul.

"Hi," she said softly.

"Hi."

"Where are you?"

"In a hallway inside the Cook County Courthouse waiting to testify," he answered. "What's going on with you? You sound a little weird."

She had to smile.

"You could tell in a few short words."

"Yeah, actually, I can. What's happening?" he asked. "Is this about George or did you rack up a huge charge card bill last night?"

"It's about George." They now referred to the case by his name.

"What about him? Are you on to something?"

"I'm not sure, but Paul, I really hate where this is heading. I mean, I really hate where this is heading."

"Where is this heading?"

"I don't want to say now. I need to check a couple of things out. I hope I'm wrong."

"Can you tell me anything now?"

"Later, when you get home. Right now, there is a big part that doesn't make sense. And I think Ed is right," she added. "I think that there is another cold case out there that this is a part of."

"It's only 9:30. How did you get to this point so fast?'

"I just talked to Saul Goldman, the previous owner. I'll tell you about it tonight. I'm still trying to connect the dots," she said. "And like I said, I hope I'm wrong."

"Something tells me that you're not."

"Can you leave after you testify?"

"Yeah, I'm out of here as soon as they let me go."

"I hope you don't have to work late tonight."

"Me too. I'll be home as soon as I can. "

"All right, see you later. Love you, Paul."

"Back at cha, Kate."

AS SOON AS SHE HUNG UP with Paul, she grabbed the cold case reports from her desk and started flipping through them. There it was.

Rabbi Lawrence Blum, age 46, Friday, September 23, 1977, shot in right side of his head, close range, car then set on fire. Bullet believed to have come from a pre-World War II German Luger.

The other documents stated what Saul had told her. He was driving in from Chicago to discuss the building of a synagogue. No witnesses. Very little forensic evidence due to the fact that the car was set on fire. Police interviewed friends and relatives. No enemies or threats. Greatly respected member of the Jewish community. Police also contacted the Skokie police, who interviewed several Neo-Nazi members. Public outrage. No leads.

Dead end. Now a cold case sitting in a stack of papers on her desk.

Kate ran up the stairs two at a time to get up to the attic. She headed toward the wooden built-in cabinet on the right and forced the door open. There sat the box. Saul was right. It was a flotsam of trinkets—a bud vase, two matching figurines of women in eighteenth century fancy dress garb, a cookbook of German dishes, an old, *Better Homes and Gardens* cookbook from 1946, a floral scarf, two matching doilies, pens, one of which was from Sullivan Ford, a wooden cross on a thin leather strap, some buttons, an old pair of scissors, keys—some small enough that they could belong to a suitcase, a small German-English dictionary from the '70s, a few English shillings.

As Saul said, it appeared that there was nothing of monetary value, but she could see that they might hold sentimental value to someone. But Lolita hardly seemed the sentimental type.

She headed downstairs with the box, knowing what her next step was. A little while later she was at the library, with the box, heading for Lolita's office.

"FOR HEAVEN'S SAKE! WHEN WILL this harassment stop?" Lolita blurted out when she saw Kate standing in the doorway of her office.

"Oh, chill the dramatics, Lolita. I'm not harassing you. I'm bringing you something that I found in the house."

Lolita froze when she saw the box that Kate placed on the corner of the desk.

"I spoke to Saul Goodman earlier today," Kate said to Lolita, who was still staring at the box.

"Who?" Lolita asked.

"Saul Goodman, the man we bought the house from. The man you sold the house to."

Lolita said nothing.

"What a nice man. He saved this box for you. He said he didn't think there would be anything of monetary value, but he thought you might still want some of these things. You know, sentimental value. He said that he tried to give this box back to you after the sale, but you refused to meet with him. Why would that be, Lolita?"

Lolita gave Kate one of her icy stares.

"Saul Goodman is a thieving Jew. I wouldn't even be in the same room with him, much less meet with him or his Jewish wife."

"That's pretty harsh."

"Harsh but true," she spat her words out. "He stole that house from me. It was worth twice as much as he gave me. Between him and his Jewish lawyer, I didn't stand a chance."

"Number one," Kate said. "From what I understand, the house was in bad shape. You couldn't even keep up with the taxes. And number two—what does him being Jewish have to do with anything?"

"What do you know about the condition of the house?" Kate saw slight shaking in Lolita's hands. "You didn't live here. You're listening to gossip from those so-called neighbors, and probably Virginia."

Kate could tell she was getting a rise out of her and just let her speak.

"I suppose you're some kind of liberal bleeding heart. The Jews are the scourge of humanity. It was because of them that the world is in the state that it's in. It's because of them that we had World War II. The world would be a better place if Herr Hitler had succeeded with his plan."

Kate could feel shivers running through her body.

"You mean the Holocaust." Kate could barely speak.

"There was no so-called Holocaust. That was all made up by Hollywood. You know who runs Hollywood, don't you. The filthy Jews."

"So six million people never died in spite of the evidence, the eye-witnesses, all those survivors."

"Absolute Hollywood nonsense. It's something that would have happened if Hitler had succeeded with his plan. There is some small truth to it, but the numbers and what has been said, well, it was all greatly exaggerated."

"I've heard about people like you. I always hoped I'd never meet one," Kate said without breaking eye contact.

It was astounding to Kate that someone could be so filled with irrational hatred and bigotry as to ignore historical facts.

Lolita glared at Kate. "You're a fool. A silly little fool."

Kate continued to look Lolita in the eyes while trying to hide the disgust she felt for her.

"Don't you want to see what's in the box?" she finally asked.

Slowly Lolita stood up and began to open the box. Kate had left everything as she found it but added a few things: copies of the pictures that Virginia gave her of Lolita's parents. She put those on the top.

Finally, Kate saw a glimmer of humanity from Lolita. Her eyes suddenly softened as she looked at the pictures. She gently touched some of the items in the box. Kate could actually see the person behind the anger and the hatred.

Kate broke the silence.

"They look so happy. I would say that they were two people who loved each other very much."

"Did you find anything else? Another box or something?"

"Of course not. I would have brought it if I had."

"This is difficult for me. Please leave my office and don't come back."

So much for the human Lolita, Kate thought.

"No thank you for bringing this to me? I could have just tossed it out on the curb for trash pickup."

"Just get out of my office."

"Gladly," Kate answered.

KATE'S HANDS WERE SHAKING SO hard that she could hardly dial the station's number. It was Roger's day off. Kelly answered.

"Kelly, hi, it's Kate. I know Paul isn't there. I'm calling to talk to you."

"Okay," she replied.

"Ed said to contact you or Roger if I need help with George."

"With who?"

"George. The guy in my backyard."

"Oh yeah. Right. How can I help?"

"Have they filled you in on the daughter?"

"Uh, yeah. Lolita. She is definitely a strange one."

"Do you know her?"

"I've seen her around and at the library. Who hasn't? She's been here forever."

"I need to find out all that I can about her. I just need a little help. It shouldn't take long."

"Okay."

"She lives in the apartment above the jewelry store on the square."

"Yes, her and her binoculars."

"Could you go over to the jewelry store and talk to the owner? I'm assuming he's the one that rents the apartment to her. If not, could you find out who her landlord is?"

"What do you need to know?"

"How long has she lived there? Any problems with her? Does she or did she own a car? Does she have a lot of visitors? Anything you can," she said. "I'll be asking around, but I think you may get more information when you show your badge. I will probably get more gossip then fact. She's not very well-liked. And it has to be a confidential conversation. I don't want her to know that we're asking about her."

"Right. We should clear this with Ed."

"Of course. Do you want me to talk to him?"

"I'd appreciate that. He's walking around like a wounded bear. He's just pissed off all the time."

"Let me handle him. Sometimes I can mellow him out."

"Please do, and I'll leave here in a few minutes."

"Thanks, Kelly. Call me as soon as you can."

"Will do," she said as she transferred the call to Ed.

"Yeah," Ed said when he picked up the call. It sounded more like a grunt then a word.

"Ed, its Kate."

"What's up? You got something for me?"

"I'm following up on something. I need Kelly's help for an hour or so. Is that okay?"

"As long as it leads to something."

"I'm cautiously optimistic."

"I need more than that, Kate."

"I think you're right, and it's connected to one of the cold cases."

"Which one?"

"The rabbi in 1977."

There was an extended silence from Ed.

"Do you know...?"

"Yeah, I know which one you're talking about," he said cutting her off. "Hope you're not grasping at straws."

"I hope I'm not either," she replied. "Ed. You okay? You don't seem like yourself lately."

"I'm fine, Kate. Just help me out here and get to the bottom of this."

"I'm trying, Ed, I really am."

"I know you are. And thanks, but I'm okay."

"Good. I'll be in touch."

"Yeah, okay," he said, hanging up on her.

SHE PLANNED ON HER NEXT call being to Virginia but decided to stop in instead.

"Hope you don't mind me dropping in," she said as Virginia opened the door.

"Not at all. Come in," Virginia replied. "Can I get you anything to drink or eat, even?"

"A cold glass of water would be great."

"Come in the kitchen and have a seat."

She went to the refrigerator and brought out a pitcher of water with just the right amount of lemons floating on the top. She poured a glass for both of them.

"So, what is the latest?" she asked Kate, making no attempt to hide her impatience.

Kate briefly related the phone call to Saul, omitting the conversation about the rabbi, but told her about the visit to the library including the moment when Lolita saw the pictures.

"That was a good move on your part. Maybe you will break down that wall."

"I saw the smallest spark of humanity in that woman today. It didn't last long," Kate said. "My blood runs cold just being in the same room with her. How do we even let her around the children at the library? She's an awful person."

Virginia said nothing. She simply nodded her head and looked out of her kitchen window.

"Did she ever own a car?" Kate asked.

"What? A car. I don't know," Virginia responded. "Let me think."

"Well, there was the big green Ford that they had when George disappeared. It was practically brand new. George would get a new car almost every year. They were his pride and joy. He would take everyone for rides in them, even us kids. Afterwards, well, it was there for years. Lolita drove it,

78

and I know that Martha did as well. She learned how to drive from George. Eventually, they had to get rid of it."

She paused to sip her water. Kate could see that she was focusing on remembering that time.

"I can remember my father taking Martha on errands, grocery shopping and such. I even took Martha to the hospital to visit a friend or relative. It was the VA Hospital on the west side of Chicago. She was so grateful and tried to pay for gas, but I wouldn't hear of it. The other neighbors took her places as well. I don't recall Lolita ever asking for a lift anywhere, but then that was something she wouldn't do."

"How long do you think that they had the car?"

"It was gone before Martha died. I think that they may have sold it to pay bills. I know Martha was starting to have health problems about that time."

She stood up and paced around the kitchen. "Let me think."

"They definitely didn't have it in 1978," she continued. "I remember because when I took her to the VA hospital that was in May of 1978. It was the day before my girlfriend's wedding. I was standing up to the wedding, and I was rushed. I was afraid that I would be late for the rehearsal."

"And Lolita never got another one."

"No, even after her mother died and she sold the house, I don't believe she did. She ended up in that apartment above the jewelry store. It's close enough to the library that she could walk to work. And the grocery and other shopping is also in walking distance, so I don't imagine that she would need a car."

"Is that when she moved above the jewelry store? After her mother died?"

"To be honest, I have no idea. I totally lost touch with her and have no idea where she went right after her mother died. I just assumed it was the apartment above the jewelry store. Sorry."

Kate refilled her water glass. They both were silent for a few moments, deep in thought.

"Did you go to the same high school?" Kate finally asked.

"Yes, but she was a year ahead of me since she was so advanced, grade-wise."

"By any chance, do you still have your school yearbooks?"

"I do. Would you like to see them?"

"Yes, yes, I would," Kate said, not surprised that Virginia would still have her yearbooks. If it had to do with the history of this town or Virginia's family, Virginia saved it, in the most orderly way, of course.

"They're in my library. I'll go get them."

As expected, Virginia had all four of them. Kate opened the one from Virginia's junior year, which would be Lolita's senior year.

"There's Lolita." Virginia said, when she saw Lolita's picture.

Kate could hardly recognize her. The picture showed Lolita with her hair down on her shoulders, a little makeup, and a smile.

"She was really quite pretty," Virginia said.

"Yes, she was. She had to have had boyfriends," Kate said.

Kate read the comments below the picture, none of them surprising. Honor Roll Student, President of the German Club. Flipping through the pages they came across another picture taken at the senior prom. To their surprise, there was a picture of Lolita dancing with a handsome young man. The comment below identified them as Lolita Schumacher and Russell Carlson, "having a wonderful time at the prom."

"Oh my gosh!" Virginia exclaimed, pointing at the picture. "Let me think. I know who he is. That's Buddy. Buddy Carlson!"

"Okay, good," Kate said. "Now tell me about Buddy."

"Oh goodness. I had no idea that they ever dated. What a surprise. How is it I never knew about this before?"

"Do you know or can you find out where Buddy is today?"

"Yes, yes, give me a few minutes and let me make a phone call," Virginia said, as she paced around her kitchen. "The coffee is fresh, if you want to switch to coffee. I'll be right back."

Kate did switch over to coffee as she flipped through the pages of the yearbook. The last few pages listed the student's names in alphabetical order and what pages their pictures would be on. Those were the only two of Lolita and Buddy. She checked out Buddy. Nothing much on Buddy other than he too was a member of the German Club. That was his connection to Lolita. He was probably an average student hoping to get through his high school days. She went back to the prom picture. Once again, she was shocked to see such a pretty and normal-looking Lolita.

A few minutes later, Virginia came back in the kitchen.

"I called my cousin," she said, excitedly. "She was in their class. Lolita and Buddy dated. It was the talk of the school for a while. It didn't last long, from what my cousin remembered. A lot of the girls had crushes on Buddy, but he seemed really smitten with Lolita. Even in high school, she was considered weird and didn't have a lot of friends. No one knew what he saw in her. But when I look at this picture, she could be quite attractive when she chose to be."

Virginia frowned and began to pace around her kitchen.

"I guess I really did steer clear of her back then," she added. "I never knew about any of this and my parents never mentioned her name. We just helped Martha out when we could."

"Where is Buddy now?" Kate asked. "And please don't say he's dead or living in Arizona."

"We are very fortunate there, my dear," Virginia replied with a smile. "He is the owner of the hardware store in Harley, a mere twenty-five miles from here."

"Trust me, Virginia, I know where Harley is."

"His father was the previous owner and Buddy took it over when his father retired. From what my cousin said, he's barely hanging on because of the big chain stores popping up all around here, but he is managing, along with his son, to keep it going. Customer loyalty and plus he knows everything about hardware and things like that."

"Well, I'm heading over there now. Want to join me?" Kate asked, knowing what the answer would be.

"Of course I do. You'll need an introduction. And this is a conversation that I wouldn't miss for anything. Let's go."

HALF AN HOUR LATER, KATE was parking in front of the old hardware store on the quiet main street of Harley, a street where many of the buildings dated back to the 1860s. This building was one of them. There was no disguising the fact that this store was old. Aside from the worn, aged façade, many of the advertising materials in the window looked like they went back to the seventies and eighties. A new ad promoting the latest in LED lightbulbs was placed in front of a yellowed, older ad promoting bug spray, one no longer being manufactured. A brittle 2005 poster from the annual parade that the town held every year lay where it had fallen years before. The windows had the look and feel of an afterthought that held no longer held any importance to the owner.

Kate was more than familiar with Harley, but she was not in the mood to share any memories with Virginia. She didn't want to lose focus today. *Maybe another time, maybe not*, she thought as they walked through the creaking doorway of the hardware store. The store smelled of age and use. The wooden planks of the floor were well worn from decades of being trod upon. She half expected to see an old brass cash register behind the counter being attended to by someone in coveralls. Instead there was a middle aged man in front of a sleek Casio register and a laptop off to his side.

"Hello ladies, can I help you?" he cheerfully asked.

Kate let Virginia take the lead.

"Well, yes, I was looking for Buddy, Buddy Carlson. Are you his son by any chance?"

"Yes, I am. I'm Cliff Carlson," he replied.

"Hello, I'm Virginia Landsbury," she said, reaching over the counter to shake his hand. "This is my friend, Kate Harrison. Your dad and I come from the same neck of the woods. My cousin Jane, went to school with him. I was a year behind. I heard he was still running this place."

"He sure is. Over forty years and he's still not ready to walk away," Cliff said.

"Really? I'm happy to hear that. Is he by any chance around? I'd love to visit with him for a short while, if I may."

"Of course. He's around here someplace. Let me find him for you."

"Thank you so much." After he walked away, Virginia smiled at Kate and gave her a thumbs up.

"Yes, great job, Miss Marple," Kate laughed.

Kate took the opportunity to walk the aisles, fascinated by the bins and shelves filled with all things considered hardware. She wondered if she needed anything for the house. It seemed only right that she buy something.

A few moments, Cliff returned with an elderly and still a very handsome man, dressed in coveralls, fulfilling Kate's imagination.

After Virginia introduced herself and Kate, she mentioned her cousin. And, of course, he remembered both of them. He seemed genuinely pleased to see Virginia. Kate stood in the background while they shared small talk. Finally, Virginia got to the point.

"Buddy, do you have a few minutes to spare?" Virginia asked. "Kate is a private investigator, and she has some questions for you."

"Does this have anything to do with the dead body that was found the other day in someone's backyard? It's what a lot of the folks around here are talking about today."

"Yes, yes it does." Kate replied, "The body is Lolita Schumacher's father."

Buddy gave a short laugh and shook his head.

"Damn. Which means you need to know about my relationship with Lolita," he said with a wry grin.

Kate nodded.

"Well, there is a bar at the end of the block. If we're going to talk about Lolita, we should head down there. I'll need a drink. Come on, ladies."

"Son, I'll be down at the corner," he said to Cliff. "If you need help with the crowds, just call and I'll head on back."

"Stay out of trouble Dad. I don't have bail money," Cliff replied as he watched them walk out of the store.

To Kate's surprise, Virginia ordered a Guiness beer. Virginia struck her as a cocktail and fine wine drinker. She ordered a root beer and Buddy ordered a vodka on the rocks. *This should be an interesting conversation*, she thought.

The bar was as well-worn as the hardware store. There were a few men, all of different ages sitting at the bar. They all made a point of greeting Buddy when he walked in. Buddy chose a table in the far corner, out of earshot from them.

"Well, what do you want to know?" he asked while waiting for the drinks to arrive.

"I'm not sure," Kate said. "I saw your prom picture in the yearbook. I know so little about Lolita and her family."

"Why do you need to know about her?"

"I need to fill in the gaps and maybe we can figure out who killed her father. And Lolita is not, how shall I put it? She's not contributing much to the investigation."

"Of course she's not." He sighed. "God, where do I begin?"

"Were you her boyfriend?"

"I'm not sure that I could be called that. We did have a relationship. We were both in the German club and had some classes together. Everyone just thought she was strange, but I was fascinated by her, had a huge crush on her. When she let her hair down, literally, and dressed up a little, she was really quite pretty. But she would have none of it. Except for prom night."

"Prom night. That seems a bit conventional for Lolita," Kate said.

"It was. But it was all part of the scenario."

"What do you mean?"

The drinks arrived and nothing was said until the waitress walked away.

"That was the night that she decided to lose her virginity. And she wanted me to be her partner. It was all very planned out and I guess the word is 'analytical'. She approached me like she was asking me to help her with a school project. She said it was time to stop being a virgin. She wanted to find out what sex was like, and she chose me as her partner. Believe me, I wasn't about to say no. I wanted to shed my virginity in the worst way. I was a seventeen-year-old with a real crush on this girl who is telling me that she wants to have sex with me. So, of course, I went along with it."

Kate and Virginia looked at each other as Buddy took a drink.

"I picked her up at her house. I even bought her a corsage. I met her mother."

"What was that like?" Kate asked.

"Her mother was sweet. Real soft-spoken and she seemed so pleased that Lolita was going to the prom. She even took some pictures. But looking back on it, there was a sadness there that to this day I can't describe.

"I didn't care, though. All I knew was that I was going to get laid. I would be a man by the end of the night, and I was with this really pretty woman, as I then thought of her."

He continued, "I had my dad's car. She had a room reserved at a hotel. We had to say that we were just married. I couldn't to this day tell you where this hotel was or the name of it. We stayed at the prom long enough to dance a few dances and ended up having that picture taken. There were a lot of shocked friends when I walked in with her. They couldn't believe it was her. She was actually smiling and talking to the other kids. And she looked so darned pretty."

He paused to take another drink, then continued.

"It was all so forced. I knew it, but I didn't care. I wanted her. I just wanted her. So we left without a lot of fanfare. We practically snuck out. I drove as fast as I could to this hotel. After fumbling around for a while, well, I guess we figured it out, and I was in heaven. I didn't want it to ever stop. But of course we had to. I got her home before dawn. Her mother was asleep."

"After that I was putty in her hands. Whatever she wanted she got, and it was usually sex. We found some of the strangest places to do it. I couldn't get enough of her. I told her I loved her because I thought that's what she wanted to hear. She laughed and told me to stop being stupid."

"How long did you have this relationship with her?" Kate asked.

"It seemed like ages, but it was probably about eight weeks. I know that it was over by the fourth of July. I was already interested in someone else by then, someone human."

"How did it end?" Virginia asked.

"She told me it was over. That we had our fun. Strangely enough, I agreed with her. I really didn't want to see her again. Sex or no sex. The whole thing was just getting too weird for me. I wanted out. You can't sustain a relationship based solely on sex. The personal part was missing. The affection. Whatever. So I said 'okay' and that was it."

"Did you stay in contact with her over the years?"

"I wouldn't say we stayed in touch. We were cordial when we saw each other. If I ran into her we chatted. Actually, once, when I was in my twenties, she saw me at the train station, and she asked me if I wanted to get laid. I just laughed. I thought she was actually making a joke. Turns out she was serious and gave me her phone number and said to call her if I did. I threw away the number."

All three were silent for a while.

Buddy continued.

"When I heard that she got involved with some Neo-Nazi group, it didn't surprise me, strangely enough. From what I understand, she was heavily involved with those crazies. There were comments that she made, when we were together, about Hitler and the Jews that kind of made me sick. But I ignored it instead of arguing with her. I figured someday good sense would kick in."

"Did the people at the library know about this?" Virginia asked. "I can't believe that they would put up with that kind of behavior."

"They didn't have a clue. Around here, she kept it under wraps. I only found out because a friend of mine, who was in high school with us, spotted her at some stupid rally in Skokie," he said. "And besides, look at her. Is she your idea of a crazed Neo-Nazi?"

"You're right. I never knew about it and I lived across the street from her," Virginia said.

"And you know, she was so disliked that I think no one ever gave her, or anything that she did, a second thought. I know I never told anybody. I could care less what she did with her life. She's just weird Lolita."

"Did she ever talk about her father?" Kate asked.

"She said hated the man. Said he was weak and a coward. She said, 'How can you respect a coward?' She didn't elaborate. She said he left them for some woman and moved to California. Aside from that, if anything was said about him by anyone, she would clam up or change the subject."

He looked around the bar, shook his head, and took another drink. Kate and Virginia said nothing.

"She appeared to be really fond of her mother though. As fond as Lolita can get with anyone," he added.

"So it definitely is her father in the backyard?" he asked Kate.

"Yes it is."

"How did she take the news?"

"Cold, unemotionally. Although she claimed that she was upset," Kate replied. "So when was she in this Neo-Nazi group?"

"In the seventies, when they started marching in Skokie. Everyone thinks that they were only crazy misguided young men, but there were a few women and she was one of them," Buddy said. "I think they may have been her only friends. What a pathetic life she's led."

"When was the last time that you saw her?"

"Yesterday."

"What?" Kate spit out. "Yesterday?"

"Yeah, she showed up with some young kid. He had purple and black hair and tattoos all over both of his arms," he responded calmly. "I asked her who he was, and she said the son of a friend. She said he was nice enough to drive her around for some appointments, and when he said he needed a few things from the hardware store she suggested coming here instead of a big box store, especially since they were in this area. And she said she wanted to stop in anyway and say hello. She was surprisingly pleasant. I haven't seen her in years, so it was a real surprise when she walked in, especially with this strange kid."

"So what happened?" Kate asked.

"What happened? Nothing happened. We spoke in generalities. She said she didn't want to discuss the situation with her father. The kid bought some stuff, and they left."

"What time yesterday?"

"Late in the afternoon." He finished his drink. "I figured that's why you showed up today, that you knew she was here yesterday."

"No," Virginia said. "We saw that picture in the yearbook and are just fishing around. Well, Kate is. I make the connections, and she does the rest."

"Yeah, well, we've taken up enough of your time. We better hit the road," Kate said thoughtfully. "Thank you, Buddy, for talking to me."

"No problem. I hope you get to the bottom of this. Let me know if there is anything else you need to know. It's not like I have anything to hide between Lolita and me. It was just a strange episode with a strange person."

"It seems that everything involving Lolita is strange," Kate added. "I do need a few things for the house, so we can walk you back to your store."

"Sure thing."

"One more question," Kate said as they headed back to the store. "Had she ever been to your store in the past to buy anything?"

"No, and I would have remembered if she had."

KATE WAS GLAD TO SEE that Paul made it home before her. He was in the kitchen microwaving leftover lasagna.

"Katie, my girl," he said when he saw her.

"Hi," she said as she walked into his arms. "Glad you're home."

"Me too," he responded. "Hungry?"

"No, I don't think so."

"You don't think you're hungry? What did you eat today?"

"A cup of coffee and a glass of root beer."

"Hmm, sounds delicious. Sit down and have a slice of lasagna."

"Okay, what about you? What are you having?"

"I'll zap another piece. You sound pre-occupied. Want to share what you've learned?"

"I will. In a minute. Let me get my notes," she said as she left the room. When she came back she began to write feverously, in between bites of lasagna. Paul continued eating while she wrote, not wanting to break her concentration.

"There," she said sighing.

"Getting anywhere?" he asked.

"Yeah, I'm getting more lost. And I feel stupid and useless."

She told him about the box and her visit to Lolita, finishing up with what she learned from Buddy.

"Interesting," Paul said, as Kate reread her notes.

"Interesting, but getting me nowhere. I've determined that she is a nasty old anti-Semitic weirdo, which is what I knew yesterday. I'm sure that she has some connection with the murder of the rabbi. I'm convinced it was her and her buddies that were involved. But how in God's name do I get any proof?"

"Find out who that kid was that she was with, for starters," he said. "I don't see her hanging around high schools and making friends with tattooed miscreants."

"Oh, and Kelly called," he continued. "Here's her cell. She said call anytime tonight. She got as much information as she could from the landlord and neighbors."

"Good. I'll call her in a little while. I'm going to find out what else I can about her mother and hopefully find some relatives."

"I think you're on the right track, Kate, but I still think somehow we have to get her to talk. She knows what happened."

"I agree. I was hoping the picture in the box might loosen her up a little."

"It still might," he said. "I'd keep a real close eye on her."

"There are still so many questions. This kid, for one, and why was she in Harley yesterday talking old times with Buddy after she left here?"

"You've shaken her up, Kate. I think it's time to really watch her."

"You mean wear a disguise and follow her around like a real sleuth?"

"Yes," he laughed. "Time for some real sleuthing, if that's a real word."

"You're right. She is suddenly on the move," she said. "I'll do my computer thing tonight and work on my disguise for tomorrow. How exciting. I get to use my binoculars and camera, like a real private detective."

"You are a real private detective and a good one," he replied. "Just be careful. I think she's really dangerous."

"So do I. Somewhere along the way, she lost her humanity."

For a few moments, neither said a word.

"What time does Nathan work til tonight?" she asked Paul while staring, once again, at the corner of the yard.

"Late, probably be home about midnight."

She said nothing, just nodded slightly.

"You okay?" he asked her.

"Yeah, I'm fine. Tell me about your day," Kate said lightly, "and then I'll call Kelly and bury myself in our library."

"Oh, by the way," she added, "I bought some stuff for the house from Buddy's store."

"What kind of stuff?"

"Garden stuff, small shovels and plants. And a birdbath for George's grave."

"HI, KELLY," KATE SAID, WHEN Kelly answered the call. "It's Kate."

"Hi, Kate," she said. "So did you solve this thing yet?"

"Very funny. I wish. What did you find out?"

"Let me grab my notes," she said. "Didn't find out too much. She's pretty boring, actually."

"Boring?"

"Yeah, I talked to the landlord, Ed Olmer, who is also the owner of the jewelry store. She's lived in that apartment since 1980 when she sold her house. Perfect tenant. Rent paid on the first of each month. He's only raised her rent three times in the thirty-plus years that she's lived there. She only pays $350.00 a month. She even cleans the jewelry store for him after hours. And then she doubles as security. If she sees anything suspicious after hours she calls him. Sometimes, the alarm gets triggered by the weather or whatever, and she calls him or talks to the cops if he can't come down there. He said he'd be lost without her. He thinks the world of her. He said she might be a little strange to some people, but he considers her a friend."

"Go figure," Kate said. "She has a friend."

"He said that twice a year, one week in the summer and then at Christmas time, she goes to stay with relatives in Indiana. Beverly Shores. She does this every year. Never changes the routine. He's never noticed any visitors, but then again, they may come in the evening when he's not around."

"No car," she continued. "Never knew her to have one. Walks to work and to the grocery store, even in lousy weather. Sometimes he drives her places if she has a doctor or dentist appointment out of town. But that's very rare. And he always offers. She'll rarely ask. She does belong to a German Club and usually takes the train to meet them at different places. She takes the train to Chicago and another to Beverly Shores when she goes on vacation. He hasn't been in her apartment often. Only when it needs to be painted or if there is a

91

repair to be made. They don't socialize, but they have a cordial relationship. Like I said, he likes her."

"Anything else?" Kate asked.

"He didn't know her before she moved in. He's not from around here. It was his grandfather's business before he took it over. He bought the business and the building from Gramps in 1979. He moved here from Sharon, Wisconsin."

"Has he heard about George?"

"Yes, he asked her about it, and she said she didn't want to discuss it. Said it was too upsetting."

"Yeah, I'll bet," Kate said. "Anything else?"

"The tenants in the other buildings next to her didn't know anything about her. None of them have lived there for very long, kind of transient from what I could tell."

"Did you by any chance happen to see a kid with purple and black hair and tattoos on both arms anywhere in the area when you were there?"

"Yeah, I did, actually. Across the street, in the square, sitting on a bench."

"Alone?"

"Yeah, why?"

"She was with him, later on in the afternoon. He drove her to Harley. They stopped in a hardware store over there and he made a purchase."

"That's kinda weird, even for her."

"Yeah, it is," Kate added. "If you see him around again, would you keep an eye on him for me?"

"Yeah, sure. Anything else?"

"No, thanks for the help. I appreciate it."

"Well, I hope it helps."

"We'll see. Every little bit, you know."

"Yeah, I know. Call me on this number if there is anything else you need me to do."

"Thanks. I'll keep that in mind," she said. "Good night Kelly."

"Night, Kate."

"SHE IS REALLY UP TO something, but what?" Kate asked out loud as she opened her laptop.

She started by looking up information on Martha, then George. She was able to find their immigration papers on the Ellis Island website. It was easier finding documentation from the late forties than from the early part of the century. Records were more legible and accurate. Martha arrived in 1946 from Germany and George in 1947 from England. She found their marriage records from Cook County. No surprises. It all fit in with what she had been told. George was listed as a mechanic, Martha as a waitress. She made a note to go to the town hall to find the birth records on Lolita. And she was sure that there would be a birth announcement for Lolita in the archives of the local paper.

She wondered where they got the money for this house. Even by 1948 standards, this was an expensive house. How did they even have enough for a down payment? She made another note to follow up on that.

She then moved on to Martha's family in Beverly Shores, Indiana. There were several families listed in the White Pages for Beverly Shores that shared Martha's maiden name. She dialed the first name listed. It was only after 7:00. She was sure any relative of Martha would want to know about this latest development. She had a feeling that Lolita didn't call them and let them know.

She was right. The first person that answered said that he was the son of Martha's cousin.

"You found George!" the man exclaimed. He sounded truly astonished after she identified herself and told him the reason for the call. "I don't believe it. How can this be?"

When she told him the cause of death she was met with total silence.

After a few moments he identified himself as Samuel. He told her that his father was Martha's first cousin. His mother, Ursula, had been Martha's best friend since childhood. They all came from the same town in Germany. Samuel told her that they moved from Germany to the United States in the late forties when he was two. His father died a few years after they arrived in the United States. Martha and Ursula were the only remaining members of their immediate families left in the aftermath of World War II. He added that they had been closer than most sisters.

And yes, he was in touch with Lolita since her mother's death, and she did, in fact, stay with them twice a year.

"I don't know what to say. I am so shocked," he said. "For all these years, we were told that George ran off with another woman. I was young when it happened, but I can remember Martha even saying that they had gotten money from him, money that he sent from California. But then the money stopped and Martha would say that he was probably dead and buried and no one notified her. In time, we never spoke about him. Not with her and not with Lolita. It was like he never existed."

He was silent for a few moments. Kate knew he was trying to absorb the news and said nothing.

"That poor man," he added. "But why would they say he was sending money?"

"Maybe whoever killed him sent the money, posing as him." Kate replied.

"That's possible. But he was such a nice man. Who would hurt him? I was very young, but I remember him well."

"What do you remember about Martha?"

"Very nice. But very nervous, very fragile, I guess that's the word that I'm looking for. Fragile," Samuel said. "Fragile and sad."

"And Lolita?" Kate asked. "How do you see her?"

"I've known her all of my life, and I still feel that I don't know her," he said. "She's pleasant enough when she is out here. She comes out twice a year. Rather distant, but polite. She spends most of the time reading or going for walks. In the summer she helps out in the garden. At Christmas, she brings little presents. Nothing expensive, but nice. But not once has she ever invited us to come up there to see her. Not that I care, but it would be nice if she did. It's what most people would do."

"What about when Martha died?"

"Oh, I remember all that very well. She called us and told us that Martha had a heart attack and died. Very unemotional about it, but that's Lolita. Very unemotional about things. We drove up for the funeral and stayed in a motel. She didn't even invite us to stay at the house, which I must say was very run down. That was the one and only time that I was ever in that house. It was a mess. Needed a lot of work. We visited for a short time at the house, and she actually said that she didn't have room for us and it's a big house."

"Yes, I know," Kate said.

"We went to a motel. After the service, we just left," he continued. "And she continues to come here every year, twice a year. We expect her to show up. We never invite her. She sends us a note telling us when the train will get in and well, she just shows up."

"When you say we, who are you referring to?"

"Oh, of course, my wife Nancy and me. I'm an attorney here in town. We don't have any children. I have an older brother, Kurt. He lives in New York. Nancy and I live very close to the house that my parents bought. It's just a few blocks away. My mother never remarried and raised us on her own. It's the house I grew up in and the house that Lolita always comes to. My mother still lives there."

"Your mother is still alive?" Kate sounding more shocked than she meant to. "I'm sorry. I don't mean to sound so surprised. I guess I assumed that she was gone."

"No, fortunately she is still with us. Going strong at the tender age of 91," he said proudly. "We Germans are a tough breed."

"I'm so glad to hear that. Do you think I can talk to her?"

"Well, tonight she's at Bingo. But believe me, when she hears this, I know she'll want to talk to you. I always felt that there was something that she knows and is not telling anyone. Martha and her were very close. She was devastated when Martha died. I think the only reason that she lets Lolita come here twice a year is because Martha would want her to. We are the only family that Lolita has. To be honest, my mother doesn't really like Lolita, and she always seems relieved when the visits are over."

"Can I have her call you tomorrow morning?" he asked.

"Oh please do. It's important that I talk to her." Kate gave him her number. "I'm an early riser, so the earlier the better. I have so many things that I want to ask her."

"I'll go to her place first thing in the morning and tell her the news," he said. "I'm still stunned. Shot in the head, you said?"

"Yes, and the bullet came from a 1937 German Luger."

"How terrible. How terrible and how confusing. I'll stay with her when she calls you. Sometimes her hearing is not so good, but her English is excellent. She is going to be so upset to hear this."

After a short pause, he asked, "And you are a private detective?"

"Yes, and for purposes of full disclosure, I do have to tell you that I'm the owner of the house now."

"Really? This is just too interesting for words," he said. "I'm assuming that many improvements have been made."

"Yes, and it looks very nice. We love this house."

"I'm glad. For George and Martha's sake, I'm glad."

KATE WAS ALTERNATELY CHEWING ON her thumb and writing in her notebook when Paul walked in with a bowl of ice cream.

"What's this?" she asked.

"Ice cream, with all those different sauces, just the way you like it."

"You are the world's greatest husband. Do you know that?" she proclaimed.

"Yes, I know. You always say that when I bring you ice cream."

"Well, you are, even if you don't bring me ice cream."

"Thanks. How's it going? Or would you rather I didn't ask?"

She looked down at her notes while eating a large spoonful of ice cream.

"I know who did it. I just know it. But it doesn't make sense until I find a reason. I know I'm not wrong about it. But until I figure out a reason, I can't say anything."

"You mean a motive."

"No, a reason. There's a difference. A slight one, but there is a difference."

"Spoken like a real non-cop," Paul said with a smile.

"A former cop, thank you very much," she said. "And it's not just semantics. There is a difference. Someday, sir, I'll explain it to you."

"When you find the reason?"

"Yes, when I find the reason," Kate continued, "Martha has a relation, a close one that is still alive and kicking. She's 91 and in good shape. I just spoke to her son. He's going to tell her about George in the morning. She's out playing Bingo right now. He'll have her call me in the morning."

"You think she knows the reason."

"She was close to Martha. And if she was as close as he says they were, then they shared secrets. Women always share secrets, especially horrible ones. Martha had to confide in her. I'm sure of it."

"It may be better if you drove down there."

"Yeah, I may just do that. With her being 91 it may be easier person-to-person," she said. "I'll see how the phone call goes."

"I think we're both thinking the same thing," Paul said.

"We probably are. I just don't want it to be true."

Kate looked away from her husband and stared at her notes.

"That's why I need a reason. A good one."

NATHAN WAS EXHAUSTED. IT WAS a busy night at the restaurant, and Jeff, the owner, kept him going. Not that he minded. He loved his job and he loved being around the chefs and the wait staff, even if he was just doing the dishes and the cleanup. The smells and activity of the kitchen, the banter between the cooking staff, were becoming a part of him. Culinary school couldn't come soon enough. He wanted to be a real part of it all.

Finding the body in the backyard had unnerved him more than he let on in front of Kate and Paul. Especially after seeing the picture of George and his wife. The image haunted him. Signs of stress were showing in Kate and Paul, as well. Kate was jittery and distracted, Paul more silent and thoughtful. He wanted this to end soon.

Nathan headed for the shower knowing that he always came home from the restaurant smelling of grease, garlic and smoke from seared steaks. After his shower, too wide awake for sleep, he picked up his copy of Shelby Foote's Civil War trilogy that Paul had given him. He learned a lot from the GED classes that he was taking, but wanted to fill in the many gaps he had in his education. So he took uncredited classes and read whatever Paul or Kate recommended, when he had the time. Now he was immersed in the Civil War.

He had only read a few pages when he was distracted by a flashing light. He ignored the first one, but the second flash made him look around. To his horror, the flash of light was a flame. A flame crawling up the corner of the house.

"Fire!" he screamed as he grabbed his phone and burst into Kate and Paul's room.

"The house is on fire! Kate! Paul! It's a fire!"

They both sprang from their bed at the same time.

"What? Where?" Paul asked, totally awake all of a sudden.

Nathan pointed to his room while talking to the 911 operator.

In the seconds after seeing the flames outside of Nathan's window, Kate and Paul sprinted down the stairs and towards the backyard, Nathan right behind them, tuning on all the lights.

Kate grabbed the extinguisher from the kitchen, and Paul headed for the garden hose. They could hear the smoke alarms going off in the house.

"Kate, aim that thing on the bottom and put out any falling embers," Paul shouted as he turned on the hose and aimed it at the flames closest to the roof.

"Nathan, see if there are any other places on fire, then get out in front until the fire department gets here!"

The flames were contained to the corner of the house, below and around the area of Nathan's bedroom. To their relief, the background noise of the sirens were getting louder. By the time the firemen got there Paul and Kate extinguished most of the flames. In seconds, once the firemen took over, the flames were gone, leaving a huge, sodden mess and a charred outer section of the corner of the house.

Kate and Paul stepped back, both wet and breathing heavily.

"Nathan. Paul, where's Nathan?" Kate asked, looking around the sudden chaos in the backyard.

"He should be out in front."

Kate ran past the firemen, over the hoses, towards the front of the house.

She saw him standing in the street near one of the fire trucks. She ran to him and hugged him tightly. He hugged her back.

"Are you all right?" she asked, her voice trembling.

"I'm fine. What about you and Paul?" she could hear the shakiness in his voice as well.

"We're okay. We're fine. Are you sure you're okay?"

"I'm fine. At least I will be when I stop shaking. And you're soaking wet," he said with a slight laugh.

"Yeah, I think Paul missed the house a few times and got me. But we're all okay. That's what matters."

"Kate! Kate!" she heard Virginia shouting her name over the din of the firetrucks. She was running towards her. "Oh my God, What's happened?"

"A fire, Virginia, a fire. It's out now. The back corner of the house. Right below Nathan's room."

"That's horrible! What happened? How did it start?" Her voice was now trembling as much as Kate's. "Is everyone all right?"

"We're fine. That's all I know right now. I'm still trying to stop shaking. Paul is back there now talking to the firemen." Kate looked around at all the neighbors that were now filing out of their homes, awakened by the flashing lights and the engine noises of the fire truck. And now there was a police squad car in the mix. She recognized both of the officers as they got out of their patrol car. They had been in their driveway the morning before.

"We're spending way too much time at your house," one of them said, shaking his head as he got out of the squad car. "Everyone okay?"

"Yeah, we're fine," Kate said.

"What happened?" the other one asked.

"A fire at the corner of the house. You can go see for yourself. Paul's in the back with the fire crew."

"No, that's okay. We're here to handle the crowd that you guys seem to constantly attract."

Another vehicle pulled up. She recognized Chris Hunter, the department's arson investigator. She met him when she was working on a case a few months earlier. She walked over to him as he was getting out of the car.

"Hey, Chris," she greeted him.

"Kate. What happened? Everyone okay?" he asked, taking in the activity around him.

"Yeah, we're fine. Paul's out back where all the action was," Kate told him. "God, Chris, I can't believe this happened to us. I know who's responsible. I'm sure of it."

"You think someone set this."

"I know someone set this."

"I'll have a lot of questions for you guys later."

"Yeah, well we're not going anywhere," she said as he started to walk to the backyard and she walked over to Virginia.

"Virginia, would you do me a favor? I know the cops are keeping everyone away, but you know these people. Would you please let some of them know that it's all okay now? Just say it was a small fire in the backyard, but everything is fine now."

"Of course, Kate. Of course," she answered as she headed towards the small group that had formed.

Kate walked back over to Nathan, who hadn't moved from the spot that she found him at earlier.

"Nate," she said as she looked around. "Keep your eyes open. I know the cops are here, but if you see anything weird let me or Paul know right away, or the cops."

"Like what?"

"Like the old lady that was staring at the house, for one. The cops don't know about her," she said, scanning the area around their house. "Or anyone weird. A young guy with purple hair. Don't make any moves or do anything. Just tell the cops or us if you do. If this is arson, and I think it is, sometimes the arsonist likes to stick around to see what the results are."

"Arson? You are kidding me?"

"No, I have a bad feeling about this. I'll be in the backyard with Paul and the firemen," she said as she walked away.

"Everything okay?" Paul asked Kate as she approached them.

"Yeah." She let out a huge moan as she looked at the damage, lit up by their flashlights.

"Let's go out front and let Chris and these guys do what they have to do."

"Okay," she answered.

"You know those embers that started falling?" he asked her, pulling her to the side of the property and out of the way of the firemen.

"Yeah."

"Well, these guys just informed me that they are pieces of rope and branches. And you can still smell the lighter fluid."

With that Kate let out a sting of expletives, interrupted only by the name Lolita.

"I'm going to see if we can get someone over to her place. We need to know if she's home or wandering the streets with some punk kid."

He headed over to speak to one of the two officers, leaving her to pace and vent her anger. He returned a short time later.

"Well, it's been a busy night in our town tonight," he told her.

"What?" she asked tentatively.

"About an hour ago the alarm went off at Olmer's Jewelry store. It was a false alarm, the lady told the cops who responded. The old lady being Lolita."

"So she gave herself an alibi. How stupid is she? Does she really think we'll fall for that?" Kate yelled.

"Calm down, Kate. We'll nail her for this."

They walked over to Nathan.

"You okay, kid?" Paul asked after giving him a hug.

"Yeah, I'm fine. Not shaking so much now. I'm okay."

"So tell me what happened. Were you sleeping or what?"

"No, I was still awake. I was still wired from work, plus I took my shower. I was reading the Shelby Foote book when my room just lit up."

"Thank goodness for Shelby Foote," Kate said, running her hands through her messed-up hair.

"Yeah, I guess," Nathan replied, suddenly realizing how lucky they were that he was at home and awake. He knew then that it could have been a lot worse.

"So you think its arson?" he asked Paul.

"Unfortunately, it looks like it. Chris, the arson investigator, will do a full report, but I'll be straight with you, Nathan. I'm sure someone set this fire."

"Why. Who would do that to us? The old lady? I don't get it."

"I think we're getting too close to the truth about George," Kate said, at the same time wondering what kind of a life they brought this kid into. Both Kate and Paul saw the fear in his eyes.

They were interrupted by one of the firemen.

"It looks like we're just about done out here. My guys are doing a walk-through in the house as well as on the outside, just to make sure that there are no hot spots or any more debris smelling like lighter fluid. Looks like it was contained to that one area," he told the three of them.

"By the way..." he added. "Is this the house where the body of that guy was found?"

"Oh yes, yes, it is," Kate said slowly. "Our neighbors are just thrilled that we moved in. We certainly brightened up their mundane lives."

"Glad I don't live on this block," they heard him say as he walked towards his truck. "We'll let you know when you can go back inside."

When Kate saw Virginia she told her to go home and get some sleep. She would fill her in the next morning.

"It's Lolita, isn't it?" asked Virginia.

"What do you think, Virginia?"

"I think it's connected to Lolita. That room, Nathan's room, used to be hers," Virginia said before she walked away.

As the firemen were finishing up, an unmarked car pulled up.

"Not a god damned dull moment with you two," Ed bellowed.

"You want to keep it down. People are trying to get some sleep around here," Paul said to him.

"What are you doing up at this ungodly hour?" Kate was glad to see him.

"God damn crime wave is keeping me up. If it isn't my hemorrhoids, it's alarms at a jewelry store or a house fire. Everyone okay here? By the way, you look like crap. Both of you."

"What can I say? Firefighting is a tough job," Paul answered.

"So, what the hell happened?"

Paul and Kate walked him to the back of the house. Nathan said he wanted to stay out front in case a kid with purple hair or the weird old lady showed up.

Paul filled Ed in, including the facts that made it look like arson.

"Well, I figured as much. You're getting too close. Someone's cage is ruffled."

"Thank God that Nathan was awake. It could have been so much worse," Kate responded, her voice trembling at the thought.

"So we're looking for a kid with purple and black hair and tattoos. Sounds like half the deadbeats hanging around the park on a Friday night."

"Yeah, I know," said Paul. "But for now, I just want to get back in the house."

Nothing more was said as they watched the neighbors slowly go back in their homes. Chris nodded to them and left. The firemen began packing up their equipment. The quiet slowly returned, as did the normal darkness of night.

Once the firemen gave the okay to go back in the house, the four of them settled in the kitchen. Paul poured all of them some wine.

Kate looked around her kitchen, surprised that the only damage inside the house was a broken window pane in the French doors that led out to the patio.

"My house stinks," she said, as she plopped down at the kitchen table.

"I'll keep the squad out here for the rest of the night. Then I'll make sure they cruise the hood as much as they can tomorrow. Someone is going to want to know if they got the job done," Ed told them.

"Nate, would you rather have a glass of milk or something?" Kate asked him.

"No, I think I need the wine. Even if I'm not so crazy about it."

"So you think it's the old hag?" Ed asked Kate.

"I know it's the old hag. First thing in the morning have someone contact Buddy Carlson, the owner of the hardware store in Harley."

She filled him in on the details of her visit with him.

"I bet the kid bought rope and lighter fluid."

Damn, why didn't I ask Buddy what they bought when I was there? Stupid, stupid, stupid. She chastised herself.

"So what did Chris have to say?" Ed asked.

"It looks like someone tied rope, with branches and probably other crap to the gutter on that corner, rope that was soaked in lighter fluid. He or she or they, lit it and took off," Paul said

"Just this one corner."

"Yep, it'll be clearer in the morning. Hard to see much right now. There may be more evidence when we get a chance to see everything. Chris said he'll be back here in the morning to finish up."

"And the hag was busy telling our guys about the false alarm. Giving herself an alibi. So she thinks that we can't even question her about it."

"That's what she thinks," Paul responded coolly.

"Back off cowboy. You're too close to the flame, so to speak. Let one of the other guys handle it," Ed said pointedly to Paul.

Paul said nothing. He just stared at his wine glass before downing the contents.

"Well, I'm heading back home and tending to my hemorrhoids. You come in late tomorrow," he said to Paul. "Our guys are outside. Get some sleep, all of you. Especially you, kid. But first take showers. You all look like crap, and you smell real bad."

"Next time we have a fire I'll be sure to freshen up before you get here," Kate said. "You'll have to see yourself out."

"No problemo," he said as he walked out.

Kate took Paul's hand then Nathan's. The three of them sat silently for a few moments.

"Nathan," she finally said. "Why don't you go sleep in the guest room? Everything is fine now. I don't want you to miss your classes or work. The only way to get past this is to do the normal things. The usual. You know what I mean?"

"She's right," Paul added, when he saw Nathan hesitate. "Go get some sleep. We'll be right behind you."

"Yeah, okay." He got up slowly and left the room without saying another word.

Once he was out of the kitchen, Kate went over to Paul and sat on his lap.

"Ed's right. You stink," Paul said holding her tightly and burying his head on her shoulder.

"So do you," she mumbled. "Oh Paul, It could have been so much worse. What if Nathan…"

She never completed her thoughts and broke off in a shudder of tears. Paul hadn't seen her cry this hard in a very long time. Sobs racked her as she dug her fingers into his back.

"Babe, it's okay. We're fine. He's fine. I'm okay," he tried to soothe her.

"Did I bring this to our front door? Is this my fault? I couldn't…I'm not…." She couldn't finish a thought much less a sentence.

When she calmed down a bit, he wiped her face with a napkin.

"Now you really look even worse." He was looking at her face smeared with soot and now tears.

Paul suddenly started to laugh.

"God, what if we were like, doing it when he burst in the room? Would he have just stood there or left the room, embarrassed?"

Kate's sobs turned into giggles.

"What would have traumatized him more, the fire or the sight of us going for it?" She started to really laugh.

"He's so polite. Would he have just cleared his throat?"

Paul began to laugh harder.

"What if you were wearing that apron and pearl necklace?"

"Or if we were on the floor…"

They both were convulsing with laughter, unable to finish a sentence.

"Or if I was, you know…"

"Can't sleep in the nude…"

They were howling with laughter as they left the kitchen to go back to their room.

Nathan, in the guest bedroom, could hear them laughing but not what they were saying.

If they could laugh, after a night like this, then he could sleep. And he did.

THE NEXT MORNING PAUL WALKED out into the backyard, coffee in one hand and his cell phone in the other. He found Kate sitting in a lawn chair drinking coffee, staring at the corner of the house.

"How long have you been up?" he asked her.

"Since five-thirtyish. What time is it now?"

"Seven. So you slept about an hour and a half?"

"Yeah, I brought our sentries out in front some coffee and let them use the bathroom," Kate told him. "It's been quiet."

"Well that gutter is shot, to say the least," he said, looking up at the twisted metal and the charred corner of the house, including a small section of the roof. "We were damn lucky that it was stopped at this point. It didn't get much of the roof."

"Why this spot? What was she trying to do?" Kate asked. "If she was really serious, why stop there? Why not other spots around the house?"

"Maybe the kid freaked when he saw the light in Nathan's room. After he lit the rope, maybe he just thought 'screw this. I can't do this' or maybe he just figured this would do the job."

"Or maybe that was all that he was supposed to do. Like a warning," Kate said. "But that doesn't make sense. Does it? She doesn't know that we know what we know. This can't be a back off kind of warning."

"In her mind, it might be. We're dealing with a nutcase here."

"Yeah, well I'll give her a call and tell her I'm done," Kate said sarcastically. "I mean, really, Lolita. It would take more than this. She's figured out that we're after her and what she knows. That's why the stupid alibi?"

Just then Paul's cell phone rang. He said a few words and hung up.

"That was Chris Hunter," he told Kate. "He'll be back out here in a few minutes."

"Don't those guys ever sleep?"

"Not when there's a fire, especially when it's a house fire and its arson."

His phone rang again—another brief conversation with Paul saying very little.

"That was Kelly. She's with one of the Harley cops. They woke up Buddy and told him what happened," he said. "You were right. The kid bought rope, lighter fluid, wire, a box of matches, and a couple of candy bars. He paid with cash. Cash that Lolita handed to him, which Buddy thought was weird. Why didn't she just pay for it? She did let the kid keep the change. "

"Bitch."

The next hour was filled with activity. Chris showed up, asked questions and took more notes and more pictures. Kelly and Roger showed up. Nathan was up and eating his cereal while filling Roger and Kelly on everything that happened. Members of the local press showed. Kate let Paul handle that. She heard him say something about the old electrical system. She doubted that they believed him.

Kate never left the lawn chair she was sitting in. She sat there watching and listening, saying very little.

Paul approached her.

"I'm not going to stay long. I need to clean up some things on my desk, then I'll be home to help with this mess and deal with the insurance guy. We need to get a tarp on that corner before it rains."

"Okay," was all that Kate said, distractedly.

"The guys out front had to leave."

"That's okay. Nothing else will happen today, except for more press showing up."

"You know the drill—no comment and send them to us."

"I will."

Paul bent down and kissed her on the forehead.

"Try to get some sleep," he told her.

"I don't think so. Not yet."

Without an argument, he nodded and walked away.

Suddenly everyone was gone. Nathan headed out for school. Roger, Kelly and Paul headed for the station. Chris told her he would be in touch. He said what she already knew. It was arson. Rope soaked in lighter fluid and wired to the gutter, debris stuffed behind the rope and at the bottom of the gutter. They were lucky that it stopped where it did.

Kate nodded and said very little.

As soon as he left, Kate walked into the house and took the stairs up to the attic.

It's the attic, she thought. It has to be the attic.

"Okay, Lolita. What the hell is up here that you wanted destroyed? What is up here that you wanted burned or so water logged that it would be ruined? And where the hell is it?"

She stood there and looked around at the empty space. She stared at the one corner that was burnt through. She could see the blue sky.

Below it, but a few feet closer to the center of the attic was the built-in cabinet. The same cabinet that held the box that Saul told her about. It had escaped the fire. A chill ran through her. *It's right above Nathan's room.*

She studied it more closely this time. It looked homemade, probably constructed by someone handy with a hammer and saw, not part of the original house plan. The entire cabinet followed the line of the attic, forming an elongated triangle. It was covered with painted flowers and butterflies. Faded with age the images could still be made out. This time when she looked inside she noticed how shallow it was. It had been big enough to hold the box, but not much more. Why build a cabinet with so little storage space, especially if it was built for Lolita's toys. Why didn't the inside follow the line of the attic, like the exterior?

There was a plywood partition—a back wall. Kate poked at it. It was shaky and not securely attached.

She looked around the attic. Nothing that could be used as a tool of any kind. So she began kicking at the plywood until it finally gave. Soon she was able to tear at the wood.

There it was, a well-worn, small, light brown suitcase with three vertical red stripes. Kate tore at the rest of the wood and removed the suitcase from the place where it had sat for so many years.

Slowly, reverently, she wiped off the dust. She knew she had found the reason.

KATE BROUGHT THE SUITCASE TO the library. She removed everything from the top of her desk and laid the suitcase in the center space. After putting on plastic gloves, she took a deep breath and opened the case.

From the inside, Kate removed two letters dated from 1938 and 1939, both written in German. One was mailed to an address in London, another had names on it and no address. There was also a pair of girl's shoes and white stockings. Underneath these items, there was a girl's dress. She recognized it as a dirndl, a traditional dress worn by German and Austrian women and young girls. This one was missing the apron—but the blouse, bodice and skirt were intact. The right sleeve was torn, almost completely off. It was decorated with a blue floral motif and was beautifully hand made. But what made Kate catch her breath was the swath of dried blood that covered most of the front of the dress.

The last remaining item in the case was a copy of *Mein Kampf*, a blood splattered copy of *Mein Kampf*.

"Paul," she heard herself saying into her cell phone while starting down at the dress.

"Kate, what is it?"

"Come home right away. Make sure Roger and Ed are with you. I found something."

"What?"

"Just come home now. I can't explain. You have to see this. Bring evidence bags."

They were there in less than ten minutes, giving Kate enough time to take some pictures and put it all back the way she found it.

"Whadya got?" Ed was the first to speak when they quickly entered the room.

Kate pointed to the suitcase.

"This was up in the attic. There's a storage cupboard that, sometime in the history of this house, was built. It's right above Nathan's room. It has a false back. I found this behind the false back. She wasn't trying to kill us or warn us. She wanted to destroy this. She must have figured the flames would get it or there would be enough water damage to render all the contents unrecognizable."

"Okay, what's in it?" Roger asked.

Slowly, she repeated what she had done earlier, laying each piece on the desk individually. First, she took out the two letters.

"Roger, we'll need you to translate these."

Then she took out the shoes and stockings, which she now noticed also had brown blood stains on them as well. She removed the drindl and laid it across the desk for them all to see.

"I'm sure forensics will find that it's George's blood."

Then she removed the bloody copy of *Mein Kampf.*

No one in the room uttered a word or even moved until Ed finally spoke up.

"That's a little girl's dress, isn't it?"

"Yes. It's a dirndl. A traditional dress worn by Austrian and German girls. And women as well. Handmade by a very skilled seamstress. They're very expensive, even today," she said softly.

She handed the two envelopes to Roger.

"Would you translate, please?"

"Yeah, sure."

"Read the one from April of '38. It's from Berlin to London."

Roger sat down in the nearest chair and gently removed the letter. He scanned the letter before he began.

My Darling Son,

I hope your journey to London was not too harsh. The crossing across the sea can be so very rough. I know how much you hated being dressed as a little girl, but we could think of no other safe way to do this. Richard had papers only for a little girl. It was the papers of a young girl who had died, and we had to make the description match. You are young enough to look like a girl when you had the wig on and wore the dirndl. In the coming months and years, you would have changed too much.

I hope someday you can understand and not speak badly of your parents who dressed you as a girl to get you out of this country. But this was something that we had to do.

Germany is a terrible place to be right now. We are on the brink of a war that will be even worse than the first one. We needed to find a safe place for you. Richard took a huge risk taking you to England. We entrusted the safety of our only child to him, and he proved to be the most excellent and trustworthy friend.

Until this awful time is over, life will be better there for you. We now have Hitler Youths that will someday fight and give their lives for that horrible man and his hateful causes. These children, children of your age, have been trained to hate and kill much like mad dogs. We had to find a way to get you away from all of this and all the suffering that is to come.

When this terrible time is over, your mama and papa will be with you again. You will probably be very much changed.

Mind Richard and his family and help them in any way that you can. I'm sure that they have saved you from a most awful fate.

Until we see you again,
Your loving Mama and Papa

"That's as close as I can get it," Roger said softly. "It's not like I get to practice German often."

"It made sense to me," Paul said.

"Yeah, me too," said Ed. "Read the other one."

"This one is dated January, 1939. From George to his parents," Roger told them, once again scanning it before reading it. It had no address on it.

Mama and Papa,

Richard told me that my last letter to you came back and never reached you. I am so frightened because I do not know where you are. Richard is doing what he can, but he told me that many people have been moved from their homes and can't be found. I am trying to be strong, but I cry at night when I am alone. I miss you and Papa so much, and I worry so much, even when Richard says that he is sure you are well.

I am helping Richard and his family as much as I can. I am learning my English, and when he has papers in German I read them to him in English. He says this is a big help in his business. He sometimes takes me to the big bank where he works. It is much like Papa's bank. I sometimes read for other people who have papers or letters written in German. I don't know who they are or what they mean. I just want to be helpful. I am trying to be as good as I can.

Richard and his family are very nice to me. They teach me many things and always in English. But I miss mama's pastries and the smell of the pipe tobacco on Papa's clothes when he would come home from his bank. I have been here so long.

Everyone here talks of a war with Germany. How can this be? They say that German bombs will fall on London. Richard says to tell people that I am Austrian. Many people hate Germans now. I don't understand. Herr Hitler is a terrible man.

I hope to hear from you soon. It has been so long since I have had a letter from you. My only wish is to see my mama and papa again.

Your loving son,
George

Roger cleared his throat as he put the letter back in the envelope. Kate wiped away tears. Ed silently looked out the window. Paul was leaning against the wall looking down at the floor. No one in the room seemed to be able to speak.

Finally Paul did.

"I'm sorry Kate, but I still don't see a reason for a 12-year-old girl to shoot her father in the head, if she, in fact did. I mean, she obviously helped move the body."

"Yeah," Ed added. "Those letters are heartbreaking, but what do they have to do with his murder? Like Paul said, she must of helped move the body."

She grabbed her notebook and began flipping through the pages.

"She told Buddy that she hated her father. That he was weak and she had no respect for him. At the company picnic, Harold said that she just glared at her father with 'what can only be described as unbridled hatred'. It was Lolita that got her mother and insisted that they…"

Before she could finish her desk phone rang, causing everyone in the room to jump.

Kate looked at the number. It was an Indiana number.

"This is Kate Harrison," she said as she quickly grabbed the phone.

"Kate, this is Samuel. I'm here with my mother, Ursula. She's anxious to speak to you."

"Hello, Ursula. Thank you for speaking with me."

"I'm so glad. I'm so glad this has finally happened in my lifetime. I'm so relieved that you found dear George," Ursula said, her voice quivering with emotion.

"Ursula, I'm here with three other detectives who are involved in George's case," Kate said to her. "I'm going to put you on a speaker so that they can hear what you have to say, if that's okay with you."

"Yes, that's fine. That's fine."

Kate was a little surprised at how slight her German accent was.

"Ursula, the three detectives are Paul Harrison, Ed Silverman and Roger Mueller," Kate added after she had the speaker on. They all greeted her.

"Can you hear us okay?" Ed asked.

"Yes, it is very clear. Thank you."

"Ursula, I want you to know that I found a brown suitcase in the attic today. Do you want me to tell you what's in it?" Kate asked.

"Nein, I know what's in it."

There was several moments of silence, before the conversation continued.

"So you found it," Ursula said. "Someone finally found it."

"What does this all mean Ursula?"

Another few moments of silence, broken by the sound of Ursula's deep inhale.

"Lolita killed her father," she responded calmly. "She shot him in the back of the head when she was twelve. She is a monster."

"Ah geez," Ed said in the background. Roger groaned something in German and Paul just shook his head.

"Oh Ursula, why?" Kate asked, trying to maintain her composure. "Why?"

"I can only tell you what Martha told me months after it happened, when she could no longer keep the truth inside of her."

"Please tell us," Kate said gently.

Ursula let out a another long sigh, almost a groan, and began.

"Martha walked in the house after work and heard the gunshot from the backyard. She saw Lolita still with the gun in her hand, wearing that outfit."

"The dirndl?" Kate asked.

"Yes, the dirndl. You can only imagine how horrible it was for her to see this. Lolita told her that her father was a traitor to Germany, a coward. She told her mother that they fought. That he hit her and tore her dress. It made no sense then to Martha, and it makes little sense to me today. It all sounded like a crazy person."

"You must understand," she continued. "Lolita was very smart. She had that book. That horrible book, *Mein Kampf*. Martha knew nothing about it. But Lolita read that book. She believed every word. That Hitler was a god. It was later that Martha found out about the book and that Lolita was reading everything she could about Hitler. You must ask Lolita. Make her explain how she could do such a thing."

"Why didn't Martha call the authorities? Why did they just bury him?"

"Two reasons—Lolita was her daughter. It was such a horrible thing, but as a mother she had to protect her daughter. It was instinct—a mother's instinct. This was her little girl. Before this, when she was younger, she was a sweet, precious thing—an only child. So bright. Lolita was everything to them. She couldn't send her to jail or a mental institution. So she panicked. The two of them just buried him. The other reason, the reason I know that Lolita is evil, is that she saw in Martha's eyes, maybe some look, something that made Lolita think that Martha would tell the police. She told Martha that if she told someone or went to the police, that she would tell them that Martha shot George because he was going to leave them. Who would they believe, Martha or Lolita? Martha would spend the rest of her life in jail, not Lolita."

"Dear God, Ursula, how horrible," Kate said. "When did you find out the truth?"

"They came for Christmas after this happened, like they always did with George. Martha looked terrible. Lolita, she looked fine. Martha could only keep up that lie for so long. She loved George so very much. So one day, she told everyone that we had to do some shopping, and we drove to a park near the lake. Then she told me. She told me the horrible truth. It was terrible. She cried so hard, I thought she would never stop. Knowing that her daughter killed her husband was horrible enough, but also, she was afraid. Afraid that her daughter would someday kill her or someone else. That's when she told me about the suitcase.

"It was her only insurance against Lolita. After they buried George and Lolita told her that she should never go to the police, Martha was still clear-minded enough to protect herself. She told Lolita to change her clothes and take a bath. While Lolita was taking her bath, Martha put the dress and the other things in the suitcase. Then she hid the suitcase in her room. When Lolita came back downstairs, Martha was standing at a fire. She told Lolita that she was burning all the evidence, including the book. She was really burning another suitcase filled with clothes. It was her own suitcase from when she came here from Germany. Lolita was angry that her mother burned the book. She never even shed a tear for her father that Martha saw.

"A few days later, Martha hid the suitcase in the cupboard in the attic. George and Martha built that cupboard together for Lolita's toys. When she was little, she used to play up there with her friends when it was too cold to go outside. Martha knew how to use a hammer and saw, so she made the board in the back. She hid the suitcase behind it. Until now.

"All of this, Martha made me swear to never tell anyone. She made me promise."

"Why didn't you go to the police after Martha died?" Kate asked.

"Martha, when Lolita was eighteen, she again begged me to never do that. She said that Lolita was fine. That she had a life. She went to school. She went to her prom. She was not dangerous. She said the Lolita was taking good care of her. Lolita didn't even go far away to college. Martha repeated this conversation with me even years later. She made me promise that I would never go to the police.

"But I was still afraid for my life and for my family. I wanted her to know that I knew what happened. I wanted her to be afraid for a change. That summer after Martha's death, she showed up uninvited. I had hoped that we would never see her again after Martha died, but there she was, just like when Martha was alive. One day I took her aside and told her I knew the truth. She acted like I was crazy, until I told her about the suitcase. I told her I knew where it was but would never tell her. I told her that I wrote a letter that would be sent to the police if I ever thought that she might be involved in someone else's death. I told her that her mother also wrote a letter, which she did, that it was in the suitcase telling the truth about that night."

"What did she say?" Paul asked.

"She said she didn't know what I was talking about. She said I should see a doctor. She just walked away. As long as George was never found, she knew she was safe. I once taunted her. She would say so many terrible things about the people that bought the house that I had to tell her that the suitcase was in the house with them. That shut her up. She knew she could never go back to look for it. I think over the years, she may have come to believe that her father really did leave them. How does one live with that truth when you are no longer a child?"

"Did you ever tell anyone else, your children or anyone?" asked Kate.

"No, no one. My son is sitting here listening to this for the first time. He is looking very shocked.

"So she comes every year, two times a year, and I breathe again when she leaves," Ursula continued. "My poor Martha, how she suffered. She was like my sister. We went through so much together."

Everyone could hear the tears through Ursula's voice.

"Where did the gun come from?" Ed asked.

"It was Martha's. Martha and I and my husband came to America together. She was single. Someone gave her the gun. I forget who. Probably a friend or relative. For protection in a strange country. Lolita, such a snoop, must have found it in their clothes closet. In a box on the shelf. Martha didn't even know it was loaded."

"Will you now arrest her?" she added. "I would be glad to know that she is sitting in jail."

"We will be going over to pick her up today," Ed said. "We will have to speak to you again, in person." He didn't want to say that he didn't know if he could get a conviction since she was a child at the time.

"That is fine with me. I want to, before I die, to look her in the eye and tell her what a devil she is."

"Ursula," Kate interjected. "You said that Martha left a note about that night. There is no note in this suitcase. There are two letters between George and his parents, the dress, shoes and stockings, but no note."

"I am not finished with family secrets, my dear. I am not finished."

"KELLY," ED SAID TO HIS detective a short time after the phone call with Ursula. "Is she still at home?" Because of the fire, Ed told Kelly to stick like glue on Ursula.

"Yeah, nothing to report. No kid with purple hair, and she stayed put."

"If she does leave, even to go buy groceries, slap cuffs on her and take her to the station."

"Really?"

"Yes, really. We'll be there in a little while."

When they got to the apartment, Ed told Kelly to call for a patrol car and wait.

"You're bringing her in?" she asked.

"Kelly, we're doing more than just bringing her in. She's getting a dose of reality."

Once again, Lolita greeted them at the top of the stairs.

"And now there are four. Plus the one outside, watching me. What is the reason for this harassment?"

"We're like the Gestapo, Lolita. We don't need a reason," Ed said looking Lolita in the eyes. "You know all about the Gestapo, don't you fraulein?"

"Lolita, this is our Captain, Ed Silverman," Paul said, pushing by her and walking into the apartment. "He's joining our little party."

Kate followed, carrying in a package wrapped in a large black trash bag. Roger close behind her.

"This is outrageous," Lolita protested.

"Lolita," Paul continued. "Shut up and sit down. I'm not in a good mood. We had a rough night. There was little fire at our house. We put it out quickly though. Not too much damage done. Your arson plan didn't work."

"I don't know anything about arson," she said. She glared at Paul, then sat down in the armchair.

"We'll find the kid, Lolita," he said. "We'll find the kid with the purple hair who bought the rope and lighter fluid from Buddy and he'll talk. He'll tell us how you hired him to start the fire. He's not going to want to go to jail just to cover your butt. He'll talk."

"I was here all night. There was a false alarm," she said, her eyes darting around the room, her posture erect.

"We know all about your feeble attempt at an alibi," Paul continued. "But that's not the reason that we're here."

"Then what is?"

Paul pulled up the chair from the dining room and sat next to her. He looked around, and when he saw that they were all seated, he looked at Lolita again.

"Lolita, tell us about the day you killed your father."

When she opened her mouth to object, Paul repeated himself, his voice brittle with restrained rage.

"I said, tell us about the day you killed your father. We've spoken to others. We know, and now we want to hear about it from you."

"Ursula, you've been listening to Ursula. She's nothing but a senile old lady," she responded, looking straight ahead. "I have no idea what you are talking about."

Paul nodded to Kate.

Kate slowly removed the small suitcase from the black trash bag. Kate finally saw real human emotion from Lolita. She saw fear.

"Look familiar?" Paul asked.

Lolita remained silent and still.

Kate opened the case and took out the dirndl, the shoes, the stockings, and the bloody copy of *Mein Kampf*.

"I'm sure that there is enough DNA evidence on that bloody dress to connect you with your father's murder. So you may as well tell us what happened." Paul said.

"So you found it," Lolita calmly said to Kate. "It was up in that cupboard, wasn't it?"

"Yes, behind a false plywood back," Kate replied. "This is what you were trying to destroy with your feeble arson attempt. How did you know it was there?"

"I saw her in the attic once. After the incident with my father. She was taking measurements. She had a piece of plywood. She told me to me to go away. That she was fixing something. I believed her. But I remembered that day. I remembered it when I stood in front of your house the other day. I knew, all these years later, what she actually was doing. She was hiding this case.

"She lied to me and said she burned it. What kind of a mother would do that?"

"Lolita, it pales in comparison to what you did to her," Roger said. "You killed her husband."

Lolita sat up straighter and looked around the room at the four of them. "He deserved it."

"Dear God," Kate muttered.

"It's time, Lolita," Paul said in a gentler tone. "It's time that you told us what happened."

She remained silent for a while. Her eyes darted around the room and finally settled on the bloody dress. A sudden gust of wind shook the front windows.

"They didn't even know that I had the case. They never knew. Sometimes I was just too smart for them. You see, they both worked. They left me alone a lot of the time. They left me to my own devices. And I was so smart. So inquisitive. One day, I found it. On the top shelf in their bedroom closet. I found the gun also. So I took it to my room and went through it. I saw the dress and read the letters. Even then I could read enough German to make out what the letter said.

"They dressed him up as a girl and sent him to live in England. Probably with some Jewish banker. And there he lived. And there he stayed while his countrymen died for Germany and for Herr Hitler. He lived a soft, easy life while others died trying to defend Germany from the Russians and the allies who were coming to destroy Germany. He was such a coward."

"He was a child. Only eleven," Kate interrupted.

"Only eleven when he was sent there. But he should have come back. He should have come back when he was older. Towards the end when boys younger then him were on the streets of Berlin shooting at the Russians. He should have come back. But no. He stayed in England, which was bad enough. And he gave aide to the enemy. He said as much in the letter. He was translating documents for them. He was a traitor to the Fatherland and to his people.

"He even talked about it at a company picnic that we went to. He wept for his parents in front of all those men. I was embarrassed to have such a weakling for a father. So I decided to confront him. I wanted him to know that I knew.

"That day, before he came home from work, I put on that dress and the stockings and the shoes. They fit me perfectly. I was going to surprise him. I didn't intend to...to...hurt him," she hesitated. "I just wanted answers. Why didn't he go back? How could he live with himself? I wanted to know about the gun. Where did it come from? Did he ever use it? Maybe if he had, I might have had a little respect for him. I was going to give him a chance to explain himself. But I also wanted to shame him. That's why I put on the dress. He needed to be shamed.

"I was in the backyard, sitting at the table, the suitcase in front of me, when he came home. She was still at work. I was reading my book. My book—*Mein Kampf.* I read it every chance that I could. They didn't know I had a copy. I found it at the library. They were going to destroy it. It was on a cart and the librarian said it was evil and would be destroyed. I took it when her back was turned. I could see that the title was German. How could it be evil? I was curious. So I stole it. The only thing that I ever stole in my life. To this day, I have no regrets.

"When he saw me in that dress, he turned white. He began sputtering nonsense. Then he saw the book. I could hardly understand him. He began to speak German mixed with English. He became crazy. I told him about Herr Hitler and how he tried to save Germany. I tried to tell him what a great man Hitler was. I tried to tell him about the Jewish problem. He slapped me in the face. They never hit me, either of them. But he slapped me. He tore at the dress. He told me to take it off. I became afraid, but I stood up to him. I told him that he was a coward. I told him he was a traitor to the Fatherland. Even though I thought he would hit me again, I confronted him. I stood tall like a proud German. He didn't know that I had the gun in the suitcase. He began to raise his hand at me again. But this time he grabbed my book, my *Mein Kampf*. Once again, he ordered me to take off the dress.

"Then he went to the corner of the yard, with my book in his hands. I saw what he was going to do. He was going to burn it. He was still rambling nonsense as he was kneeling and making a pile of leaves. Then he reached into his pocket for the matches. That was when I assassinated him. I had the gun in my hand. If he would have turned around I would have just threatened him, but he didn't turn around. I had to stop him. Besides, it's what would have happened during the war if he had been discovered giving aide to the enemy.

"She walked in just then. She made such a scene. I'm surprised the neighbors didn't hear. But it was October and cold. Windows were closed. And then we buried him. That was the end of the story until now, of course."

Her next remarks, slathered with contempt, she directed at Kate.

"You just had to dig him up, you little bitch. You couldn't just leave well enough alone. You think you are just so smart, don't you? Well I'm sure I can't even be arrested. I was a child at the time. A confused child defending herself from an enraged parent. So this has all been a waste of time."

Ed spoke first.

"And then you went on with your life and hating Jews, doing what you could to contribute to the final solution."

"Yes, that's one way of putting it. The truth must stay out there. People must not forget how evil the Jew is—how he controls the financial markets, how he will destroy Christianity, if he is left unchecked."

"And you became a member of the American Nazi Party, didn't you?" he asked.

"Of course. Like I said, the truth must stay out there. Americans are so pro-Israel, so pro-Jew, someone must be brave enough to tell the truth."

"Lolita," Ed continued. "September of 1977, a rabbi by the name of Lawrence Blum was murdered in his car. The car was then set on fire. He was on his way here to have a discussion about building a synagogue here in town. Do you know anything about this?"

"Yes, I do."

"Tell us what you know."

"The young man with the purple hair is the son of Frank Wadell. Frank and I are both members of the Nazi Party and have been for years. I met him in Skokie when I went there to go to school. I chose Skokie so that I could see firsthand what the Jews were up to. We marched together several times. We were also lovers. Unfortunately, Frank was stupid and several years ago killed someone in a silly barroom brawl, so he's sitting in jail. I do keep in touch with him and his son.

"When we heard about the plans for a synagogue and we acted upon it."

Paul had seen this type of behavior before. She was boasting. She was proud of what she had done.

"By murdering the rabbi?" Paul asked.

"Someone had to. We couldn't let them do this. A synagogue would bring more Jews into the area. We couldn't have that," she calmly responded. "And it worked. To this day there is no place for the Jews in this town to congregate and do whatever it is that they do in their so-called places of worship."

"Since you're in the mood, please tell us about that night," Ed said with a catch in his throat.

"It was common knowledge among the Jews in the area when he was coming and where he was coming from. It was easy to get the information if you just kept your ears open. When the day came it was just a matter of waiting on the side of the road. One of the other members had been following him, and we knew what kind of car he had. So I simply played the damsel in distress and parked my car on the side of the road with the hood up and lights flashing. The car was on just enough of an angle so that anyone coming by would have to slow down or stop. Several people did. I simply said the tow truck was on the way.

"But when it was him, it was really quite simple. I went over to talk to him and Frank shot him in the head from the passenger side. Frank was even able to get his hands on a German Luger. We then set the car on fire. And we went home. But not after making love for hours in the forest preserves as a way of celebrating.

"I proudly admit doing my part for the cause. Is there anything else that we need to discuss?" she asked to the stunned group in front of her.

"Yes, there is, Lolita. Yes, there is," Paul said.

He once again nodded to Kate.

Kate sighed and looked at Lolita, who was now focusing on the view outside the living room window.

"Lolita, listen to me," she said to the woman.

Lolita broke her gaze and slowly turned her head toward Kate.

"Lolita, you are a Jew," Kate said as clearly and forcefully as she could.

"That's utter nonsense. Why would you even say such a thing, you stupid person?"

"Because it's true. You are a Jew. You come from a long line of Jews. Your grandparents on both sides died in concentration camps at the hands of the Nazis because they were Jews."

"You are insane. I go to a Lutheran church. I was raised as a German-American. Don't talk so crazy. Why would you even say such a stupid thing?"

"We had a long talk with Ursula."

"I told you, she is senile. She has dementia. And you are stupid enough to believe her ramblings."

"Lolita, she told us about this suitcase. If you had looked at it a little more thoroughly, you would have seen that the lining of the lid has been hand sewed to the edge. If you had cut the thread this is what you would have found."

Kate slowly let part of the fabric fall. She removed a yellow, fabric Star of David, a yarmulke, a photograph of a young boy, and three documents. They included a German birth certificate, German papers with a photograph of a young girl, and a letter written in English by Martha.

Lolita stared down at the items. There was a sudden pronounced tick in her left cheek.

"This is the Star of David that your father had to wear, designating him as a Jew. This is his yarmulke, and this is a picture of him at maybe the age of ten or eleven, with very black hair," Kate said, taking out each document slowly and placing them on the table. "The first document is a letter written by your mother detailing the events of the night that you killed your father. It was her insurance as well as Ursula's in the event you murdered someone else or even threatened to."

The three documents were encased in clear plastic folders that Kate put them into before they left the house.

"This is the document showing your father dressed as a young girl, which got him into England.

"And this your father's birth certificate. Roger please translate some of it and show it to Lolita."

Kate could see Lolita's hands start to tremble.

"Once again, this is nonsense. I am not a Jew."

Roger began to read.

"George Schumacher, born May 21, 1927. Parents Jahn and Frieda Schumacher of Berlin, Germany. Jude."

"You know what Jude means, don't you, Lolita?" Kate asked, handing the document to Lolita. "It means Jew. Look for yourself."

Lolita could barely hold the document with her shaking hands.

"This must mean something else. Some kind of forgery," her voice became frantic and quivering.

"No, Lolita, you are a Jew. Pure and simple. This is what Ursula told us," Kate began.

"The reason that your father was sent to England dressed as a girl had nothing to do with him having to fight for Hitler. It had everything to do with saving his life. His parents saw what was happening to Jews across Germany. His father was a banker, the most detested of all Jews, and his mother was a professor of literature, another detested profession. They must have known even in 1938 that their days were numbered, so they contacted a British banker that worked with his father, your grandfather, over the years. He agreed with them about what was happening in Germany at the hands of Hitler and the Nazi Party. He also agreed to take George to England. They knew of a family who had recently lost their daughter several months before, and he used her papers to get George into England. He told officials that she was an orphaned niece and he would be adopting her. The ruse worked in both countries.

"George's parents, these people who sent your father away so that he would be safe, your grandparents, both died in concentration camps: your grandmother at Auschwitz in 1941, your grandfather later in 1942, after doing slave labor in Dachau. Here is the documentation that I pulled up on the internet. But most of this information came from Ursula."

"NO! You're liars, all of you! Get out of here, you filthy liars!" screamed Lolita, throwing the document that was in her hands at Kate.

"Your grandparents on your mother's side fared no better," Kate continued calmly, ignoring Lolita's outburst.

"Your maternal grandmother died after being subjected to medical experiments at another prison camp. God only knows what kind of torture that poor woman endured. Your maternal grandfather was never found. He was last seen also doing slave labor at the Krupp's ammunition plant."

"Shut up! Shut up, you stupid person. None of this is true. I was never told this. It is not true. They simply died in the war. No one knew what happened to them."

"That brings us to the next point," Kate went on as if delivering a lecture to a student.

"Ursula and your mother were very close. They both suffered so much at the hands of the Nazis. They too were in prison camps?"

"That's not true. That's not true. That's not true," rambled Lolita.

"Your mother had a scar on her left arm. That was from the painful method that was used to remove her number. It was acid. Both your mother and Ursula evaded the Nazis until near the end of the war. They were eventually found and sent to Dachau. Ursula didn't get into many details. That's for another time. Luckily for them, the Allies arrived in time, and both girls survived. They had lost their families, but they had survived.

"When they eventually got to America, they made a vow. A vow stating that would tell no one that they were Jews. They knew what they had suffered. They also knew that anti-Semitism was prevalent in America. They refused to suffer anymore at the hands of those who hated Jews. They refuse to let their children suffer any of the discrimination and hatred that was still a part of the American culture. Their religion and their culture was a burden that they wanted no part of. So they shed it and became American citizens, Lutherans who had emigrated from Germany. They would have nothing to do with Judaism. They would tell their secret to their children when they became adults. At that time the children could decide how they wanted to live their lives."

Kate paused long enough to see the horror now etched on Lolita's face.

"When your mother and Ursula got married their husbands agreed with them. Someone had mentioned to me that your father had a funny nose. That was from a bad nose job that he subjected himself to so that there would be no suspicion of his heritage.

"The secrets were kept, for so many years. Your father never got a chance to tell you the truth. And later your mother was too scared to tell you the truth. She lived her life afraid that her daughter would murder her as well."

Lolita began to shudder. She tried to stand up, but Paul put his hand on her shoulder, forcing her to sit back down.

"So yes, Lolita, you are a Jew. You have hundreds of years of Jewish blood running through your veins. You could very well be a direct descendent of Abraham.

"You are a Jew, Lolita." Kate repeated. "You are a Jew."

"Liars, liars, this is some kind of trap! I am not a Jew!" Lolita screamed. She clawed at her arms, as if something could be removed if she clawed hard enough.

"Take a look at the documents, Lolita. Take a look and see if we are making anything up. You are the very Jew that you despise so much. If you had lived in Germany during the war, you would have likely suffered the same fate as your grandparents."

"This can't be happening. No, it's not true!" she screamed, wide-eyed, spittle forming on her lips. She reminded Kate of a caged, rabid animal.

"Oh it's true, sister. It's true," Ed said standing up. "Lolita, I now have something to say to you. So get a grip.

"I also am a Jew. My name is Ed Silverman, and I come from a long line of proud Jews. I remember very well the night that the Rabbi was murdered. I remember it too well. So I say to you, in memory of all of my Jewish family and friends as well as in the memory of Rabbi Lawrence Blum, you are under arrest for the murder of George Schumacher and for the murder of Rabbi Lawrence Blum. You have the right to remain silent."

"Don't touch me!" she shrieked at Ed when he approached her.

Paul lifted a screaming Lolita from her chair by her arm. He let Ed put on the handcuffs as he continued to recite her rights.

When they got her down the stairs, her protests could be heard by everyone on the street as Kelly and Ed got her in the patrol car.

Back upstairs, Kate tried to get to everything back in the suitcase. Her hands were trembling so severely that she let Roger take over. Paul reached out and took her hand. He gave Roger unnecessary instructions on what to do with the suitcase as they walked downstairs; all the while Lolita's screams bellowed in the background.

Neither said a word as they watched the patrol car drive away.

"Come on, I'll take you home," Paul said.

"No, no, that's okay. I'll walk. I have to shake this off. I'd rather walk. And I have to tell Ursula and then Virginia."

"I'll call Nate," he said "I'll be home as soon as I can."

Kate nodded and began to walk, then run in the direction of their house. Paul watched her until she was out of his range of vision.

VIRGINIA WAS SITTING ON HER front porch when Kate got there. She sat down in the opposite chair and held her head in her hands, saying nothing.

Virginia also said nothing, sensing that something serious occurred.

When she raised her head and looked at Virginia all that she said was, "She's been arrested."

Virginia sat in silence.

Kate briefly told her what happened.

"My God," she finally said. "How blind were we? How could this have happened?"

"How different do you think it would have all been if she never found that book?" Kate asked.

Virginia nodded, lost in thought, as she stared over her front lawn.

"There are no answers to some questions, Kate," she finally said.

Kate stood up. "I'm going home. I'll talk to you tomorrow."

She walked slowly to her house, stopping to look at the trampled lawn and broken shrubs from the night before. Once inside, she opened some windows hoping the foul smells from the night before would dissipate.

Then she went in her library and called Ursula.

"She's under arrest, Ursula. She's been arrested."

"Thank God. Danke, Kate, Danke. Thank you," she replied so softly that Kate barely heard her.

"You're welcome, Ursula."

With that Ursula hung up.

Kate went into the kitchen and poured herself a glass of wine. She brought the bottle with her as she headed for the living room, sat down on the couch and waited for her husband.

A short time later, Paul walked in with Ed and Roger. No one said a word as Paul walked over to the cabinet that held the scotch and poured the three of them a drink. He sat down next to Kate.

"How's Virginia?" Paul asked breaking the silence.

"Rattled."

"How are you?"

"Rattled, but all right."

"Did you talk to Nathan?" she added.

"Yeah, He's picking up a pizza on his way home. He should be here soon. He's not at the restaurant tonight."

"How is she?" Kate asked Ed.

Ed finally spoke.

"You don't see foaming at the mouth too often. But she was foaming at the mouth and losing her mind."

"Her screaming really got on my nerves," Roger said.

"She'll end up in a padded cell before long," Ed added. "But she's the DA's problem now."

"Do you think they'll get a conviction?" Kate asked.

"We picked up the kid, so we'll get her on arson," Ed answered. "We should be able to get her on the rabbi. Don't know about her father. She was a kid. Like I said, she the DA's problem now."

"Where is she at now?"

"Someone gave her a sedative to calm her down," Paul said. "We called in a public defender. She was in her cell talking crazy when we left."

"Need another glass of wine?" he asked her.

"Yes, but I'm too tired to get up and pour it. I don't know when I'll be able to move again."

"Rog, pour the lady a glass of wine," Ed said to Roger.

"Sure," he said, getting up and taking her glass. "Anyone else need a refill?"

Paul and Ed handed him their glasses.

"So tell me, what is the difference?" Paul asked Kate. "Between a motive and a reason?"

"She was a child. Children don't have motives. They have reasons," she answered.

"Good job with this, Kate. Thanks," Ed said.

"I didn't do much. It was Ursula and the suitcase. I really didn't do much."

"And you found both, hon," Paul said to her, taking her hand. "To me you're still the best PI ever."

"Why do I feel so miserable?"

"Because you always feel this way after a real ugly case. It has something to do with facing evil," Paul said. "You get depressed."

"Yeah, don't look too deep at these dirt bags and nutcases. Otherwise you'll end up nuts like them," Ed added.

"Wow, Captain, that was profound," Roger commented sarcastically, handing Ed his drink.

"Hey, I didn't say nothing dirty," Ed answered.

"I said profound, not profane."

"I know what you said, rook," Ed said. "And I was talking to the lady. Don't let it get to you. You did a great job. Move on and shake off the bad stuff. You did right by George and Martha."

"Maybe I should get out of this business. Maybe get a real job, like a bank teller or a receptionist," Kate said.

"I hear there's an opening at the library," Paul said with a straight face.

They were still laughing, and not sure why, when Nathan walked in with the pizza.

"SO TELL ME AGAIN," PAUL asked Kate a couple of days later. "Why are we inviting half of the town over to our house after the funeral?"

"Because," Kate replied, fixing Paul's tie, "It's customary to have a luncheon after a funeral, and Virginia's already done enough just planning this service. It's the least we can do to help. Did I tell you that she even found a rabbi who will say a few prayers in Hebrew?"

"Yeah, you told me. It's a nice touch. But you know a lot of the people who show up are just going to be curious about the house and George."

"I'm sure there will be some of that, but there will also be the people who as kids knew George as Santa and Martha as the lady at Woolworths. These people have fond memories of them. And for a short time, even pleasant memories of Lolita. Then there are the people who actually worked with George. They're up there in years, but they still remember him. Remember, I spoke to two of them."

"How much food did we order?" Paul asked as he zipped up the back of the black dress that she had slipped into.

"Enough for fifty people."

"Hope it's enough," he said. "We do have a few cops coming, you know."

"Hmm. Maybe I should call Jeff and change it to seventy five."

"Well, let's go and get this over with."

"I'm proud of you and Nathan, offering to be pall bearers. It's really a sweet thing to do," Kate said as they walked down the stairs.

Nathan was waiting for them at the front door.

"Oh Nathan, you look so handsome in that suit," Kate said as she smiled proudly at him.

"Yeah, I know. I'm a real babe magnet at funerals," he replied, with a timid grin.

"So, who are the other pallbearers?" he asked Paul.

"Ed, Kelly, and Roger," Paul answered. "I don't know who the sixth one will be."

"Buddy," Kate interjected.

"Really? That's good of him," Paul said. "Heck we might not even need six. It should be a light casket."

Nathan grinned at Paul. "It will be a closed casket service? Right?"

"I hope so," Paul replied. "I've seen enough of him as he is now. Although that would really draw a crowd."

"His bones won't be rattling? Will they? That would creep me out."

"Hell. That would creep me out too," Paul laughed.

"Enough! Can we please go now?" Kate asked, opening the door. "Ghouls, the both of you."

As they walked near the church, stepping over cables from the news media vans and trying to avoid reporters, Kate spotted an elderly lady holding on to the arm of a younger man. She knew it must be Ursula. While Paul and Nathan went over to the hearse to where Buddy, Kelly, Roger, and Ed stood, she approached the couple.

"Ursula? Samuel?" she asked. "I'm Kate Harrison."

"Kate, Kate Harrison," Ursula replied, but the rest of what she said was lost on Kate because Ursula responded in German.

"Ma, English, please," Samuel said.

"Oh, I am so sorry. Sometimes I get confused. Since talking to you, I've gone back. I'm back in Germany with Martha, and I think sometimes I can't come back."

"That's okay. This must be a very emotional and difficult time for you. But I am so glad that you could come. Seeing you today makes me feel even closer to Martha and George. Through all this, well, it's like they've become my friends."

"You would have liked them, Kate," Samuel interjected, "I have such good memories of them. They were nice people, happy people who liked to have fun. They deserved better."

"But, Kate, if not for you," Ursula said reaching out to hold Kate's hand. "Samuel and I would not be here at George's funeral, a funeral that he should have had so many years ago. And that monster would not be in jail."

"Mom, please," Samuel said. "Let's not mention that person. Not now."

"Ursula, if not for many things. I played a small part and maybe I got some help from George, who wanted the truth to come out."

"And it was you Ursula," Kate continued, "You had the courage to finally share what you held inside of you all these years. You had to go back to such a painful time. It's all so tragic."

"Yes, yes it is," Ursula said with tears in her eyes and still holding on to Kate's hand. "So very tragic."

"Would it be all right if I sat with you?" Kate asked.

"Yes, I would very much like that," Ursula said, looking at the crowd that was converging on the church.

"Let's go inside," Kate said as she led them up the stairs of the church, still holding Ursula's hand.

George's casket stood in the center aisle. Ursula and Samuel both laid their hands on it and bowed their heads, as did Kate. She led them to the front pew. Soon after, Paul and Nathan joined them, and brief introductions were made.

Virginia sat across the aisle with Rose Cummings and Harold Simmons, George's coworkers from Sullivan's and another gentleman whom Kate didn't recognize.

The service was emotional, considering, or because of, the circumstances of George's death. At one point, Kate turned around to see that the small church was entirely filled, with many people standing in the back or upstairs in the balcony.

After prayers by the minister and eulogies by some of the townspeople who remembered George, the rabbi entered the church. He made a small statement in English, but it was the prayers he said in Hebrew that struck the emotional chord with so many. It was the rich, poetic character of the ancient language, which brought many to tears. Ursula and Samuel both wiped away tears, the personal tragedy of it all resonating the most with them.

Soon after, the pallbearers carried George to the waiting hearse. Not a word was spoken in Kate's car as they drove the few miles to the cemetery.

She watched as her husband and son assisted in carrying the casket to George's final resting place, next to his wife. After another prayer by the minister and one by the rabbi, George was lowered into the ground. Those surrounding the grave were slow to walk away, still lost in thought.

"You will come to our house, won't you?" Kate asked Ursula and Samuel when the crowd began to finally disperse. "I would really like to visit with you."

"Of course," Samuel answered, holding his mother's arm. "Of course, but we want to stay here for a little while longer." Ursula said something in German as she looked back at George's grave.

"There's no hurry. Come over when you are ready."

"Kate, we better get to the house before the throngs of people get there," Paul said.

"All right, let's go."

Once back in the car, Kate looked back at Nathan. He hadn't said a word since they left the house.

"You okay, Nate?"

"I guess so. I just am so sad. After what everyone was saying, I feel like I knew the guy. Any way that you look at this thing, it's just so freaking sad."

"Yeah, it is, Nathan," Paul responded. "It's just so freaking sad."

Nothing else was said on the drive home.

KATE WAS GLAD THAT SHE had called Jeff, Nathan's boss at the restaurant and the caterer, and had the food order increased. A lot of people were walking into her house. Nathan went to help Jeff as soon as he walked through the door. Paul tried to stick close to Kate but was approached by so many people that he hardly had a chance to get himself a beer. There were a large number of city and county cops, as well as city officials that showed up. And they all wanted details and a look at the former grave of George's, which was now covered with a birdbath and flowering plants.

She was glad to see that Brad, the coroner, and Chris, the arson investigator, took the time to come to the service. And she finally had a chance to talk to Virginia.

"It was lovely, Virginia. It really was," Kate said. "You did a great job on such short notice. I just can't believe all the people that showed up. It's amazing."

"He really was well-liked. And all the publicity had a lot to do with it," she replied, looking around at all of the people filing into Kate's house.

"I have someone that I want you to meet," she added, taking Kate's hand and walking over to the house library.

"Kate, I'd like to introduce Saul Goldman, former resident of this lovely house."

"Kate, I am so glad to meet you," said the handsome older gentleman.

"Saul, what a surprise. You flew up here on such short notice to be here. I can't believe it. It's so nice to meet you," Kate said, sincerely pleased.

"It's nice to meet you, too. It just seemed like something I had to do. Can't explain it," he said. "By the way, I love all that you did with the house. It looks great. It's in good hands."

"It's a bit tainted, but we love it and we're going to do all that we can to make the ugliness go away."

"I do have something to tell you," Virginia interjected.

"What?"

"At the cemetery, I was approached by Lolita's lawyer. She gave me a check, signed by Lolita, a check to cover the funeral expenses."

"Really?" Kate paused. "Why does that make me want to cry?"

"I had the same reaction," Virginia said. "And it's more than enough to cover today and keep the gravesites in flowers for a while."

Kate couldn't respond.

"I went to see her," Virginia added.

"You did?" Kate asked, somewhat surprised. "How is she?"

"Despondent, but lucid. She actually seemed glad to see me. She's on suicide watch at the hospital. I think every day she has another revelation on how she ruined her entire life as well as the lives of her parents. I couldn't help but feel sorry for her. I didn't stay long, but I did tell her that I would come back to see her again. That made her smile."

Kate left the library with promises from Saul and Virginia that they would stay for a while.

As she walked through the growing crowd in her house, she saw Ursula and Samuel in the foyer.

"Would you like a tour?" she asked them.

"We would love a tour," Samuel said. "This is not what I remember from my last visit."

"It is what I remember," Ursula said, looking around. "It's what I remember from when they just bought the house and from the time that Lolita was a little girl. Yes, I remember a lot of happy times in this house."

"Did you know how they came to buy this house?" Ursula asked Kate.

"No, but I have to say, I did wonder about it. Even in their day, it was an expensive house."

"Richard, Richard in London," Ursula said.

"The banker that got George out of Germany?" asked Kate.

"Yes, that one. He always kept in touch with George, always helped him, a wonderful man. He was like a father to George. When he died, he left George money, enough for George and Martha to buy this house.

"So you see, Kate, there are many good people in this world," she added.

"Yes," Kate nodded. "Yes, there are. Let me take you upstairs. I have something for you. Are you all right with the stairs?"

"I'm fine. I'm still healthy and strong."

After Ursula showed Samuel the two guest rooms, she asked Kate not to open the door to the room that Lolita once had, now Nathan's room. Kate took them into her room. She had Ursula take a seat by the window while she went and took a small box from the closet.

"You both should have this," Kate said to the elderly woman. "Some things should not be forgotten, even if they're not good memories. It's part of your family's history."

Ursula looked at the small box and ran her hands slowly over the lid before opening it. Inside were the documents and the yarmulke that were in the suitcase, as well as the original photographs that Virginia gave to Kate. The letter written by Martha was included. Kate also included the tie clip that was found on George.

No one spoke as Ursula slowly looked at each item.

"Danke, Kate, danke," was all that she said.

"I'll leave you both. Please stay here until you feel ready to come down. It's a little crowded and crazy down there right now. We'll talk more later on."

Once downstairs, she walked through the crowd in her house. Once again, she was amazed and touched by the people who came together for George. Grabbing a glass of wine, she stood by the entrance of the living room. Paul was standing by the fireplace being questioned by two very senior citizens. She watched as he politely answered their questions.

He looked up, and when he saw Kate he raised his drink in a toast.

She returned the toast and took a drink of the sweet white wine. It was a short time later, while chatting with a neighbor, that she heard a familiar British accent coming from the direction of the front door.

"Something tells me that I missed a missed a major event while I was across the pond."

"Terrance!" she said as she ran into his arms. "You're home. Oh my God, you're home."

"Yes, love, I am. And it appears you have quite a bit to share with me," he said, returning her hug.

"I do. I really do. Oh, I am so glad to see you. I am so very glad to see you."

They were soon joined by Nathan and Paul.

"All is well," Kate thought happily as she watched the three of them exchange greetings and laughter. "All is well."

Made in the USA
Middletown, DE
09 October 2016